HOME FOR
CHRISTMAS

By
John Cody

Note for Librarians: a cataloguing record for this book that includes Dewey Decimal Classification and US Library of Congress numbers is available from the Library and Archives of Canada. The complete cataloguing record can be obtained from their online database at:

www.collectionscanada.ca/amicus/index-e.html

ISBN 1-4120-4847-8

Printed in Victoria, BC, Canada

 Printed on paper with minimum 30% recycled fibre. Trafford's print shop runs on "green energy" from solar, wind and other environmentally-friendly power sources.

TRAFFORD *Offices in Canada, USA, Ireland and UK*

This book was published *on-demand* in cooperation with Trafford Publishing. On-demand publishing is a unique process and service of making a book available for retail sale to the public taking advantage of on-demand manufacturing and Internet marketing. On-demand publishing includes promotions, retail sales, manufacturing, order fulfilment, accounting and collecting royalties on behalf of the author.

Book sales for North America and international:
Trafford Publishing, 6E–2333 Government St.,
Victoria, BC V8T 4P4 CANADA
phone 250 383 6864 (toll-free 1 888 232 4444)
fax 250 383 6804; email to orders@trafford.com

Book sales in Europe:
Trafford Publishing (UK) Ltd., Enterprise House, Wistaston Road Business Centre,
Wistaston Road, Crewe, Cheshire CW2 7RP UNITED KINGDOM
phone 01270 251 396 (local rate 0845 230 9601)
facsimile 01270 254 983; orders.uk@trafford.com
Order online at:
trafford.com/04-2655

10   9   8   7   6   5   4   3   2

HOME FOR CHRISTMAS

Acknowledgements

- With special thanks to Emma Power for her constructive criticisms and her support. Without it the book wouldn't have been possible.
- My brother Jim for his fantastic art on the front cover.
- My dear friend Dan Horgan for his financial support as well as his continued support.
- All my co-workers at Elm View Court Developments, their support was much appreciated.
- And to Pat Mc Donagh for his encouragement.
- To the Writers Academy in Wexford, for the formatting of the book along with their helpful suggestions.

CHAPTER ONE

Mary Flynn sat alone in her little cottage at the foot of Mount Leinster. Her Husband, Seamus, had just left for work at the local mill, when she heard the Dog barking. She got up and went to the back door, opened it and let the dog in. The dog followed her into the kitchen and sat down, watching Mary as she filled her dish with food. Mary put it on the floor beside her and the Dog started eating.

Mary had the flu so she took some tablets the Doctor had prescribed for her earlier. The Dog started barking and ran to the front door. She was wondering who on earth would be calling at this hour as she went to answer it.

"Hold on there a minute till I put this Dog in the kitchen," she muttered to herself.

When she finished, she opened the door. She got a terrible shock when she saw a young Guard, standing outside.

"Mrs. Flynn, it's about your Son, Michael." He spoke softly as he took off his cap.

"Oh please, don't give me bad news. Tell me, have you have found him?"

"We aren't sure. That's why I'm here."

"Well, you had better come in." As she walked to the sitting room, she felt frightened and wished Seamus was there with her. "Please do take a seat," she said gesturing to the armchair.

The Guard took off his cap and placing it on the floor, sank into the seat with a well-rehearsed sigh. "There was a body taken from the Barrow early this morning. That's the reason I'm here."

"Oh, God," Mary went cold, "and you are sure that it's my Michael?"

"We aren't sure, that's why I'd like you to have a good look at this." Taking a chain with a medal on it from his pocket, he handed it over to Mary to look at. "Have you seen it before?"

"I'm not too sure, but I know that my eldest Son Patrick had a few like this one." She turned it over in her hand. "Father O' Leary brought them home from Lourdes to him."

"And where is your Son at the moment? We would like him to see this medal."

"He is away in College but he could be home at the weekend. What has this medal got to do with anything?" Mary handed it back.

"It was around the neck of a young boy's skeleton. Two fishermen found it, caught up in a bough below the riverbank."

"Where have you taken the remains?" she whispered.

"We've had them removed to Dublin for identification. We are hoping to get an analysis of the bone structure so we can try and find out his proper age. How long is it now since your Son disappeared?"

"It will be going on three years this October. He would have been seventeen at Christmas."

"Well, don't give up hope but it will take us about a month before we know anything."

"Why will it take that long?"

"We will have to search every town and village and the full length of the river Barrow for any more clues. Trying to establish if it could be another boy could prove to be exhausting."

"What happens if there is no other boy reported missing?"

"Then we will have to assume that it is your Son and his remains will be brought here."

"You will keep in touch in case there are any new developments?"

"Yes, of course! I will leave you with the medal so that you can show it to your Son."

"I will let you know the minute I see him, but there are hundreds of those medals about."

"Well, I will leave you now as we have a lot of work to catch up on. Will you be all right, Mrs. Flynn?"

"Yes, I just have a heavy dose of the flu. It's hard to shake off in this cold weather." He got up to leave and she too got up, escorting him to the door. "Goodbye now, Mrs. Flynn. I will keep in touch."

She watched him go out the gate and down the lane that led back into the village. She then closed the door, and went into the kitchen. She was still shaking so she took some more tablets with a glass of milk. When she finished, she knelt down and said a prayer. After she finished, she went to the cabinet and took out the key to Michael's room. Just before she got to the bedroom she took a glimpse into the mirror in the hallway. These past three years have taken its toll on me, she thought to herself. Her young image was now replaced with wrinkles and gray hair. Worry had left her three stone lighter, however her own image was the least of her worries.

She opened the door and went over and sat on his bed. After a few minutes the Dog came into the room and sat down beside her. She looked around his room and saw the fishing rod that he made standing up in one corner. She remembered how it took him two days to make it and how happy he was the day he came home with the finest two trout you had ever seen.

The new bicycle she had bought for his birthday was still in its wrapper; he had never seen it as it arrived two days after he had disappeared. On top of his wardrobe was his photo looking down at her. He still had that cheeky grin since he was a little boy. She got up and took the photo down as tears came to her eyes.

"Where are you, my little wild boy? Oh, why can't you come home?" she sobbed, "I miss you so much, Son."

Mary lay down on Michael's pillow, holding his photo tightly to her chest. The tablets were taking effect now and as her mind drifted back to happier times, she thought of the day she gave birth to her first Son. Her Husband Seamus had gone to work, while her best friend, Sally Mulhall stayed with her. When her waters had broken, Sally went for Doctor Byrne and then on to get the local Midwife, Molly Casey.

When the doctor arrived he'd told her that it wouldn't be long till she gave birth. Through her pain she saw Molly arrive at the door, wearing a blue shawl with a long dress and no stockings. She noticed that, oddly, the Midwife was wearing a pair of men's shoes that were too big for her. She was old, toothless and decrepit.

Mary had had to stifle a laugh when the old toothless Midwife had told Sally to stop scratching her arse. "Get the hot water and towels in here straight away!"

Sally had filled the basin and got the clean towels for her.

"Now, both of you get out and let me do my job," Molly shouted both at Sally and the doctor. "And don't forget to put on the water for a nice cup of tea when I am finished!"

The baby was arriving, and Molly was shouting at Mary to push harder. "Come on now, take a deep breath. Go on now, push like hell!"

She continued to encourage Mary. "That's good, Mary, the head has appeared! One last big push!"

"Oh God!" cried Mary. "I can't. I've no more strength!"

"Come on now, love. Try. One more hard push! God, this is a tight little fecker but we'll move him!" Molly paused to wipe her hands on a towel. "If I had a penny, Mary, I'd put it between your legs, this one's so mean that he'll come out for it," she laughed. "Get ready now and push, that's it, all over!"

She took the child, held it up and smacked its bottom. The baby let a roar.

"It's got a good pair of lungs anyway! A grand healthy child." Molly took the child and wrapped it in a towel. Mary, looking exhausted, had asked quietly, "Is it a boy or girl?"

"Well, replied Molly, "The pump is here but the saddle is missing! You have a beautiful Son, congratulations!"

"Oh thanks very much," said Mary excitedly.

Handing him to Mary she said, "This boy is thirsty now, so put him on one of those tits!"

"I am feeling very thirsty myself," Mary replied, "Could you ask Sally to bring me a cold glass of milk?"

"I will send in the Doctor first, to make sure you are all right. I will go and have a cup of tea myself and the best of luck with your Son, love."

Molly walked into the kitchen while the Doctor and Sally were sitting down drinking tea. She let a shout at the Doctor: "Get up off your fat arse and see to that girl!"

"And you," talking to Sally, "your friend would like a glass of cold milk! Don't worry," she continued, "I can make my own tea. Is there any nice soft biscuits about?"

"Try that press over there," said Sally as she filled a glass of milk. Sally followed the Doctor up to Mary's bedroom. When the Doctor came out, he told her that Mary had had a baby boy.

"Oh, that's great news!" she said as she walked in. "Good on you, girl! Gimme a look! God, he's so beautiful! Have you picked a name for him yet?"

"No, I'm leaving it up to Seamus! I will name the next one."

"That Midwife is half-mad. Did you see the state of her?" asked Sally. "Ah, her bark is worse than her bite but she is first class at her job."

Mary yawned. "I'm feeling dead tired now so I am gonna have a sleep. Wake me up when Seamus comes in!"

"I will, but he won't be home till about six thirty. I'll make you a nice bit a dinner." Sally left the room, and went in to join the others in the kitchen.

"How many is that you brought into the world?" the Doctor was asking Molly.

"It's my first one here in the village. In London, I lost count after a hundred!"

"Where did you work in London?" inquired Sally.

"In St Mary's hospital in Paddington, I also did my training there".

"I was told that you bought old Jamie Murphy's cottage in the village. Is it true that you are single and have plenty of money? You must have paid a good price for that cottage," said the Doctor, jeeringly.

"Well, let me tell you now, baldy. First of all, whatever money I possess is my business and secondly, I was married. He was a no good bowsie who wouldn't work on batteries. He would lie about all day and all he wanted was beer and cigarettes. It wouldn't have been too bad if it was out of his own pocket but it wasn't!"

Molly wet her lips. "He often came home and threatened me and one night he made a swipe at me. It was the last swipe he ever made I can tell ya! I downed him with the frying pan and I haven't seen him since. And good riddance to him. I found out after that he had another woman behind my back! Anyway, I have Polly now and that's all the company I want."

"Is Polly related to you?" asked the Doctor.

"Are you trying to take the piss out of me? Polly's me talking budgie. I took him home from London with me and he's the smartest bird you could ever lay your eyes on. The best bit of company anyone could have."

"I'm so sorry if I offend you but I've never heard of a talking bird," said Doctor Byrne.

"Well, that's because you have never travelled! Anyway you'd sink a ship with that weight, you must be at least twenty stone," she smirked.

"Giving or taking a few pounds. I am trying to lose weight. My Wife and I go for walks at the weekend," the Doctor grimaced, patting his belly. "Anyway, how do you get around?"

"I have my pony and trap. Well, I had better be going. I can't be like you two sitting around on my arse all day!" She got up and left telling Sally to keep an eye on the baby.

"She really has a sharp tongue. Some of these days she is going to cut her own throat," said the doctor. "No wonder the Husband left her - on a dark night she'd frighten the shit out of you! Well, I better be off myself as I have a good few calls to make. Tell Mary I will call in tomorrow!"

"Goodbye now, Doctor. I'll see you tomorrow."

Sally woke Mary at six o'clock. "Well, how are you feeling now?"

"I'm feeling a lot better. That sleep has done me a power of good. I'd love a cup of tea!"

"I will get it straight away and I'll make you a nice chicken sandwich while I'm there."

She returned after a while carrying the tea and sandwich on a plate. "The men'll be here any minute now! I better go and put their dinners out. You know them. They're always starving. I'll call back in later and bring you some dinner."

"Thanks, Sally. I would have been lost without you!"

Sally just had the dinners on the table, when she heard the men coming. She went out to greet them. "Had a hard day?"

"Not at all, but we could eat a baby's arse this minute!"

"Well, I hope it's not your son's!" Sally laughed. "You're a Father, Seamus!"

"You're joking?" Seamus beamed from ear to ear.

"Come in and see for yourself!"

"Did you hear that, Joe? I'm a Father!"

"Congratulations, Seamus. I hope you have many more!"

"Well, you better go in and see your child! I have your dinners ready for you's!" said Sally as they both walked into the room.

When Seamus saw the child he was overwhelmed. "Thank you, love! He's beautiful!" "Indeed he is," said Joe, "a fine healthy boy!"

Seamus looked towards Joe and said, "When are

you and Sally going to produce a baby? You's were only married a year after us?"

"They're expensive Seamus, we'll be taking our time".

Sally came in and asked the men into the kitchen for their dinners. Seamus was too excited to eat.

"I thought you were hungry?" she scolded him.

"I am, but this child took the hunger off me!"

"But we are going to have a few drinks to celebrate? Have you picked a name for him yet?" asked Joe.

"I am leaving that up to my sweetheart. God, Joe, I dunno what to call him!"

"Well, it's March and Paddy's Day is near!"

"You're right! So let's call him Patrick Joseph Flynn."

"Would you like that name, love?"

"Of course, it's a lovely name and he's even called after you, Joe, that's wonderful."

"Joe, I'd be honored if you and Sally would be his Godparents," said Mary.

"We'd be delighted to do it for our best friends."

Seamus asked Sally and Joe to stay the night and they both accepted. After the men had their dinner, he cycled to the pub. It was not long till he came back with enough drink to celebrate for the night.

Sally started to tell them about the midwife and the carry on with Doctor Byrne.

"She told us that she has a talking bird, a budgie, and it was called Polly!"

"She must be around the twist. I've never heard of a talking bird!"

"Neither have I," replied Joe. "What made her pick this village? That cottage she bought cost a few bob!"

"Well, my Father was telling me that both her parents are buried here! He remembered them well. He was telling me that the night she was born. Her poor mother thought Halloween came early!"

"Why was that?" inquired Seamus.

"Well," said Joe laughing loudly, "Because she was so ugly! She was also married in London. He was no good so he left her! Would you blame the poor chap? Sure, he must have had nightmares sleeping with her."

The child was christened two weeks later by Father O'Leary in the little village church. Afterwards, Seamus invited his friend's back to his cottage for a party and it went on till the early hours of the next morning. The next evening, Seamus told his Wife that he was glad there was such a good turn out the night before.

"I wish John had been here," said Seamus.

"You miss him a lot don't you?" replied Mary.

"He reared me ever since our Parents passed away and made sure I was set up before he went to America. You would have loved him, Mary. He was great fun."

"I would have loved to see him but some day I will get to meet him."

"Yes, I hope so. He could be married himself and cannot afford to come home."

The following year, Mary gave birth to another boy. The Doctor advised her not to have any more children. It would be too dangerous for her, as this child was nearly the death of her. She survived and the child was christened Christmas week. She named him Michael John Flynn. Joe's Parents stood for the child, and they had another good night back at the cottage.

Mary would have loved to have a little girl, but it was never meant to be. She was happy with her two Sons, and thanked God for sparing her life.

The years passed on and soon it was their first Son, Patrick's, first day at school. She was worried about him because he was such a quiet child. Michael kicked up a fuss, as he wanted to start school himself, and he began to cry.

"Ah, don't cry, Son. You will be going next year," she had reassured him.

"But Ma, I want to go now with Pa."

"And who will look after me? I would be left all alone in the cottage with no-one to talk to."

"All right, Ma, I didn't think of that! Can we go and feed the ducks instead?"

"Why not? I'll get a loaf of bread and we can go for a walk up the Barrow. There's nothing to do at home and we can collect your Brother on the way back."

She bought the bread and got a few packets of sweets, and walked up towards the river. "Look over there at that big building!"

"Where, Ma?"

"There in front of you."

"Oh ye, I see it now."

"Well, that's the Christian Brother's School and when you get older you will go there." "Will Pa go there too?"

"Yes, sure, he will be there before you."

"He won't be, Ma, cause I get up earlier than him! I will be there first."

She smiled and looked down at him. He was such a handsome child.

When they came near the riverbank, a piebald horse was tied to a tree.

"Look Ma, the horse, I am going to get one when I grow up. It's a nice horse, Ma!"

"It is indeed! And look over there!" she said, pointing to a foal. "That's her baby."

They walked up further, and saw a barrel wagon caravan and three people sitting down. There was a man and woman and a young boy around Michael's age.

"Good morning" said Mary as she was passing. "It's a lovely day!"

"It is indeed, Mam. Are you taking your boy for a walk?"

"He wants to feed the ducks!" shouted the young boy.

With that Michael said to the boy, "What's your name?"

"Miley," replied the child.

"That's a nice name. My name is Michael and I am going to school next year, aren't I, Ma?"

"Yes, of course. Now leave the nice people in peace!"

"They want to know everything at their age, Mam. Young Miley here is the same."

"Well, I suppose they learn that way. He's not shy like his older Brother. He's so quiet! Well, I better be off. It was nice talking to you. Come on Son or all the ducks will be gone."

"Goodbye, Michael. Have a good time!" the travelling man said.

"We will!" he shouted back. When they reached the Barrow track, the ducks and two white swans were on the far side. "They're too far away, Ma," he said disappointedly.

"Not for long," Mary said, handing him the bread to throw in to the river. When he threw the bread into the water, the ducks flew over followed by the swans.

The swans were taking most of the bread and that got Michael angry. "It's not fair, Ma, if I had a gun I would shoot them. The little ducks are getting nothing."

"You can't shoot them or they would put you in jail. They are a protected species." "Well, why can't they put the swans in jail and then the ducks would have plenty to eat?" After a while he got bored. "Come on, Ma, will we go home?"

"It will be too early to collect Patrick so we will go home and have a cup of tea first." On the way back, they stopped beside the camp, and Mary handed Miley a bag of sweets.

"Thank you very much, missus. Did you see the ducks?"

"Yes, indeed I did."

"He wasn't too happy with the swans taking all

the bread," said Mary. "We will be seeing you as I have to collect my older son from school. It's his first day."

"Thanks for giving the young lad the sweets," his Father replied.

When they reached the cottage, she made tea and sandwiches and had a little rest.

"When are we going for Patrick?"

"We are going in a minute."

"Ah, hurry up, Ma."

They walked back into the village, and he was waiting at the gate. Patrick's eyes lit up as he ran to greet them. "Hi ye, Ma. Hi, Michael!"

"Well, how was your first day?" Mary said, kissing him on the cheek.

"It was great!" he replied. "I have Sister Bosco and she is very nice and we had great fun all morning."

"That's great. I brought Michael up to feed the ducks to pass the morning. We were talking to Miley and his Dad, and we seen his horses and the baby one."

"Who is Miley, Ma?"

"They're travellers who have camped up near the Barrow track." Hand in hand, they walked back up through the village, to their cottage.

Chapter Two

The following year Michael started school and he shared a desk with Miley. At the break no other boys would play with Miley.

"Why won't the other boys play with you?" Michael asked.

"I'm a traveller and they don't like us."

"There is nothing wrong with being a traveller."

"They call my Dad tinker Dan because he likes to mend pots and pans."

"Well, I like your Dad and I will play with you and be your friend."

"Thanks, Michael."

After school his Mother was waiting for him, and seen him walking out the gate with Miley. "Well, how did you get on son? I see you met your young friend again."

"The other boys won't play with him because he's a tinker. Isn't it wrong, Ma?"

Patrick came out, and as they walked by the gate, Miley was standing alone by the wall. He looked lost, so Mary went over to him.

"Don't worry, sweetheart, in time you will have good friends. Give them time and you will see I was right. Look, here comes your Dad now."

Miley ran to meet him.

"We meet again, Mam. Sure, it's a grand day."

"They won't play with Miley, Dan," added Michael.

"Don't be calling the man by his first name. Have a bit of manners."

"I am sorry, Mister."

"Not at all, you call me Dan anytime. I would prefer that."

"I will always be Miley's friend and I will play with him."

"That is very nice of you. At least he has one nice lad to take care of him. Well, we had better be going."

"It was lovely talking to you again and don't forget what I said Miley!"

"Good luck to you, Mam, and to you, young men."

On the way home, Michael asked,

"Ma, why does Dan have twine holding up his trousers?"

"Because he might not be able to afford a belt. They are very poor."

"Are we poor, Ma?"

"Well, we're not rich but we are better off than a lot of people."

Their conversation was interrupted by an awful commotion at the other end of the village, with Midwife Molly and Doctor Byrne.

"Look at that poor pony; his feet are off the ground. He doesn't know if he's coming or going. Get down, you big heap of shit and walk with that pony before I report you for cruelty. You should be ashamed of yourself."

"This is the only way I can make my calls," replied the Doctor.

"Well, with your weight you should have a stronger horse. Or maybe an elephant would be better for you."

A young Guard came on the scene and Molly laced into him. Mary walked on with the boys who were laughing their hearts out.

"She's mad, Ma, and ugly," said Michael.

"Don't let her hear you saying that or she'll go mad."

It took a while for the other boys to take to Miley. But in the end, he had loads of friends, and Michael was his best friend.

"Your Mother was right when she told me that some day I would have loads of friends. She's a very nice lady."

Patrick would be getting his first communion in May, and their Mother told them that she would take them to Dublin to buy clothing for it. The day finally arrived and they were delighted to take their first trip away from the village. When they arrived in Dublin, they got on a bus and went upstairs. When it took off, Michael said, "This bus will crash."

"What makes you think that?"

"Sure there's no one driving it, Ma."

She laughed and then explained that it was driven from downstairs.

"What does that mean?" he asked.

"Well, it can carry more people than a single bus, just watch out for one passing. See - that one stopped there. Now, there's the driver."

"Oh yeah! I see him now, Ma!"

When they got off, they walked around the city, and were so excited, looking at all the stuff. They would never see that many shops in the village. It was great. When they were finished, she brought them to the zoo. They saw all the animals and were delighted looking at the penguins and the way they walked.

"They would remind you of the Nuns," Patrick said. "But not Sister Bosco, because she wears all white. Why is that, Ma?"

"It's because she is a Novice. That means she's training to be a Nun." She got all his clothes, and bought some Dublin rock, for Seamus, Joe and Sally.

"I am buying some for Miley, Ma"

"That's very good of you. Here's another six-pence."

It was late when they arrived home and they were only fit for the bed.

It was the first Saturday in May, when Patrick got his First Holy Communion. He looked lovely. He was wearing long trousers and a blue blazer, a white shirt with a red tie; he looked like a little angel. The Nuns brought them into the school for a little food. He got plenty of money and on the way home; he bought himself a saving box, and put the rest of the money into it. His Dad and Joe went into the pub and came home locked. The two of them fell asleep on the floor. The boys got up early for Mass and their mother and Sally took them to Bray for the day.

When they arrived home, the men were still drunk and the boys went to bed after an exciting day.

It was coming up to Christmas and their Father took both of them out into the woods, to collect holly and cut down a nice Christmas tree. When they got back to the house, they had great fun decorating it. They hung the holly around the walls and put decorations and balloons on the ceiling. They had just finished when Mary reminded Michael that it was his birthday on the following Friday.

"You're a lucky boy as Santa will be bringing you something as well."

"That's great, Ma. I'm gonna get double presents."

"I have invited Joe and Sally to spend the Christmas with us"

"We'll have a great time, Ma. It's the best time of the year, Ma, and I love it."

During their dinner Michael became inquisitive and asked his Father if the Nuns were bald. "I don't really know, son. Who told you that?"

"The lads at school told me."

"What do you think, Joe?"

"Well, Michael, do you see that turkey?"

"Yeah," replied Michael.

"Well, the Nuns are as bald as his arse!"

"Is that right, Dad?"

"Well, if Joe tells you, it must be right, Son."

Laughter crowded the kitchen. It was a great Christmas, and they were looking forward to next year.

They started back to school after the New Year, and it was pelting snow. The boys had great fun throwing snowballs, and making snowmen in their front garden. It lasted over a week and they were disappointed when the thaw arrived. Patrick became an altar boy and he loved helping out Father O' Leary in the church. March was a bitter cold month with plenty of frost. The boys enjoyed it as they would pour water on the path outside Molly's home and then slide up and down on it. That was before Molly came on the scene.

"What are you doing? Are you's trying to kill me? You little baskets. I've a good mind to cut the arses off you with my blackthorn stick. Go home and pour the water outside your own doors."

The lads ran away and from a safe distance they watched her put salt on their slide.

"The rotten ugly cow, I hope she breaks her neck before the frost goes!" exclaimed Michael.

They all picked up a stone, and pelted her door and then ran like hell. It was the end of April and their Mother brought them to Dublin again to buy

Michael's clothes. He would be getting his first communion the following Saturday. When she had everything got, they took a walk around the city, where they came on a pet shop.

"Look at the puppy in the window. He's beautiful and what lovely eyes he has. I wonder what would your Father say, if I bought him for you?"

"What can he say if we bring him home?" said Michael cheekily. "Tell him it's my dog and I wanted you to buy it for me."

She liked the dog herself so she went in and bought it. It was a pure bred collie. They had great fun with the pup on the way home.

When Seamus saw it, he too was pleased. "Ah, that's a lovely little pup. What are you going to call her, Son?"

"You mean she is a girl?"

"Of course she is!"

"Well then, I'll call her Lassie"

"That's a grand name. It suits her."

"That will be her name then, and when she gets bigger we will make her a dog kennel in the back garden."

It was Michael's big day and he felt so proud walking into the village, with his Mam, Dad, and Brother Patrick.

Joe and Sally were waiting in the church, along

with his Parents, who stood for Michael. He wore a beautiful fawn suit and blue shirt with a white tie to match. When they came out of the church, it was back into the school for something to eat. The moment he set eyes on Miley, he went over to him.

"Where are your Mam and Dad?"

"They're waiting outside for me."

"You look great in that suit!"

"Thanks, but it was the nuns who dressed me."

"Did you get much money?"

"I got sixpence between my Mam and Dad."

"I've got loads of money. Here, stick that half crown in your pocket!"

"Ah, thanks, Michael!" he said.

Mary was wondering where Michael had gone and then she saw him with Miley.

"I am going over to see Michael's friend."

"Sure, I will go with you," Seamus replied.

When they went over Mary told him he was beautiful and handed him a half crown. "Thank you very much, Mrs. Flynn"

"Well," said Seamus. "Are you going to introduce me to your friend?"

"Miley, this is my Dad."

"I am pleased to meet you, Son."

"Thank you, Mr. Flynn."

"You look grand, are your Parent's not with you?" Seamus said while taking out two shillings to give to him.

"They are outside waiting for me and thanks for the money"

"Well, enjoy your day!"

"See you, Miley!" they called as they walked away.

"Wouldn't you think his Parents would stay with him."

"Ah," said Mary, "He's a little traveller. Don't be passing judgments"

"Do you think it is wrong for him to be going around with our Son?"

"No, I don't," said Mary, looking stern. "He's is a grand lad!"

On the way home Michael bought sweets and comics and the men went for a drink.

Dan directed his son go in to the shop to spend his sixpence.

"I have more than that," said Miley, while showing his Father the money.

"Where did you get all that?" said Dan, looking stunned. "I hope you didn't rob it!"

"I didn't, Dad. I got it off the Flynn's".

"Bring him home, Maggie. I' m going to find out the truth."

Miley started to cry.

Mary and Sally were in the kitchen, and Michael and his Brother were playing with Lassie. There was a knock on the door and Mary went to answer it. Dan was standing outside.

"I am sorry for troubling you, Mam, but my lad tells me that you gave him some money. I'm afraid in case he stole it. You know what young boys are like. I don't want to see him get into trouble."

"Miley would not do that," said Mary. "Yes, we gave him a few shillings"

"What am I going to do now? I accused him in the wrong."

Michael went to the door and heard Dan's voice.

"Hello, Dan! God, you look lovely in that suit!"

"Well, I better go home and apologize to him."

"Hold on a minute, Dan," said Mary as she went inside. She came back out with two full bags of things for him. "For you and your good woman and there is some things in the bag for Miley."

"Thank you ever so much, Mam, and thank you, Michael."

"Have a good night, Dan."

"Well, goodbye now and thank you again."

"Goodbye, Dan."

He walked out the gate and Michael shouted at

him to tell Miley that he would see him in school. When he got back, Maggie was sitting by the campfire and the kettle was boiling.

"Where is he?"

"In there, crying his heart out. You spoilt his day."

"I am so sorry."

"Well, go in and tell him that, the poor creature."

Dan got up into the caravan. He heard Miley crying. "I am so sorry, Son, for accusing you in the wrong!"

"Why would you not believe me, Dad?"

"I am afraid for you, Son. I don't want you going through what I had to bear in that industrial school. I love you with all my heart, please forgive me Son."

"Was it that bad in there, Dad?"

"It was a living nightmare. Some day I will tell you all about it."

"Oh Dad, I love you," Miley said throwing his arms around his neck.

"I will never doubt you again, son. We will go out and join Maggie at the fire. Mrs. Flynn has sent you up something." They went outside. "Look at all the drink, Maggie. We will have a whale of a night."

"And I got minerals sweets and cakes."

"That woman is very fond of you, Son."

"She is a lady, Dad, and Michael is my best friend. Ma, you hold on to this money for food."

"No, Son, it's your big day and it was given to you."

"But I insist. You two have already given me everything I need." She eventually took the money. "Will you sing for me tonight, Ma?"

"When I get a few of these bottles into me, I'll sing all night for you"

So they had the best night in years, thanks to Mrs. Flynn.

Seamus and Joe decided to go into rearing pigs as the government had started a new scheme. They would send you a sow, already serviced. The first litter would pay for the Sow, and then the rest would belong to them. They worked on the old pig shed at the back of the cottage and made it suitable for the arrival.

They had already applied for their first venture into pigs and she would arrive on Monday evening. They were all excited waiting for the sow to arrive, and when she finally came they were overjoyed. They put her into the sty and Lassie was barking at her like mad.

"I think that she's jealous Joe."

"We better go in and get her some pig meal."

So off they went to Pat Carpenters pub. He sold anything that was needed. He was a General Merchant.

"Give us a pint while we are waiting."

"You should give her some stout. It does them wonders," said Pat.

"Pat, that would cost us a fortune."

"No, it won't. I will keep all the slops for you. You can collect the barrel every Monday; I'll leave it at the side for you. You just mix it through the pig meal and make it very sloppy"

"Thanks, Pat."

They brought the meal home on the crossbar of the bicycle. They fed her and watered her for the night.

"We will have to get a few bales of straw somewhere to keep her dry."

"Jim Walsh might give us a few."

"We will call to him on our way home from work. We should be able to carry two each."

They arrived home with the straw and cleaned out the sty and made her a nice bed. When they got the barrel of slops, they mixed too much stout through the pig meal.

"What's wrong with the pig, Joe?"

"She doesn't seem the best. I will go and get the Vet."

The Vet came and introduced himself as Dan Horgan. He was a big man with a strong Kerry accent. Upon examining the Sow he pissed himself laughing.

"What's the matter with her?" asked Seamus, looking confused.

"You fucking idiots! There is nothing wrong with her at all! You got the poor fucker drunk!"

They saw the bright side and started to laugh themselves. From then on Mary kept a close eye on her during the day as she was due her litter anytime. Young Michael came in from school and his mother had his dinner ready. After he had eaten it, he got up.

"I am going out to check the Sow, Ma."

"Good lad, keep an eye on her"

It was not too long later when she had her first piglet and Michael was amazed.

The Sow started to eat them and Michael was wondering what was happening. The piglets came out one way and then went back in through her mouth and then they came back out again. I better go and tell Ma, he said to himself, looking for back up. So he went in and told her that they were going in and out.

"Oh holy god, she is eating them!"

She rushed out to the pig shed. Michael followed her but she could only save six of them.

"Say nothing to your Dad. He will kill both of us and say nothing to Patrick."

"Why, Ma?"

"Because Patrick will tell him."

"Don't worry, Ma. My lips are sealed."

When they came home that night, Mary broke the bad news to them.

"Oh, she only had six. She should have had at least a dozen."

"Well, that's all she had. I was watching her."

"That won't pay for the Sow. We will have to sell her and the piglets. Even then we are going to have to add a few more bob to that ourselves."

So that finished the pig business, they lost more than they gained. It was coming up to Patrick's confirmation so once again they went to Dublin. After Mary had bought everything she needed, she took them up to the top of Nelson's pillar. They looked down on to the streets and everything looked so small that it was breathtaking. It took them a while to come back down as Mary was tired.

"Sit down and take a rest."

"Where are we going then, Ma?"

"I have to go to Moore Street."

When they felt better, they walked on further. They got to Moore Street and they enjoyed the way the hawkers shouted out their prices.

"Lovely apples - two pence each. Ripe bananas - four pence a pound. Come and buy some."

When they got back home, they were worn out from all the walking and went for a sleep.

Patrick got his confirmation, the following week. Mary and Sally took them to Bray. She had their photos taken in a professional studio and the boys were chuffed.

"I will send them to you as soon as I can. Just leave me your address," said the gentleman. They had a smashing day at the seaside and when they arrived home, their Dad was in bed.

"Goodnight, Ma. Thanks for a great day."

"Goodnight, boys and pleasant dreams!"

Patrick was thirteen now and Michael would be twelve this coming Christmas. They were off school now for the summer. Patrick spent all his time helping Father O'Leary. He was getting old now and a new Curate would arrive in September to help him carry out his duties.

Michael decided to go and see Miley because he got bored sitting around the house. He was half way there when he heard barking behind him. Looking back he could see Lassie running towards him. She jumped up on him and started licking him.

"How did you get out you little scamp? Come on

then, you might as well come with me. Anyway, Dan and his family would like to see you."

When he reached the camp, they were all sitting around the fire, having their breakfast. "Well, holy God, how are you Michael? Sit down here and Maggie will make you a cup of tea. That's a lovely dog you have there, what's his name?"

"It's a girl, Dan, and I called her Lassie".

"A great name for her, come here girl."

Over she went to Dan and sat beside him.

"I am going up to check the nightlines, Dad."

"Be careful along that track, it's full of holes."

They went along the riverbank and every now and then, Miley would stop and pull in a line.

"How many do you set at a time?" asked Michael.

"About a dozen."

"Here you pull in this one, you might be lucky."

"There's something on it. I can feel it!"

As he pulled it there was a swish in the water.

"Look, Miley, what is it?"

"Look, it's a big rainbow trout. Pull like hell, Michael!"

He got the trout out on to the bank, and Miley took out the hook. It was about two pound weight. "Is that good?"

"If we could get a few like this, they would make a grand supper."

"This is great sport, when do you set them again?"

"Not till evening, come on and check the rest."

When they were finished they had two trout and four eels. They were very slippery, just like snakes.

"But they're lovely when they're fried up in the pan with a pinch of salt."

"Would you like to come fishing some day?"

"I would love to but I have no rod."

"Either have I. I made up one. I will show you how to make one."

"That's great. We can have good fun."

When they got back to the camp Miley showed Michael his homemade fishing rod.

"It's easy to make."

He walked back with Michael as far as the village.

"Don't forget what I told you. I will see you tomorrow. Good luck, see you Lassie."

Michael watched Miley until he was gone out of sight. When he reached home, he told his Mother about the nightlines and how he was going to make a rod.

"Will you buy me a cane in Pat Carpenters?"

"I have a few empty tread spools that you can have. Jimmy Griffin sells hooks and line so you will have your rod in no time."

"Thanks, Ma."

"How did Lassie get out?"

"I was half way to Miley's and she was behind me barking."

"I seen her jump the gate after you left. She's very fond of you. You may take her with you when you go away again."

"I will, Ma. Dan and Maggie say that she is a lovely Dog and they're going to try and get one for Miley."

"That would be grand. Sure, he must be lonely without any Brothers or Sisters. You take care when you're up that Barrow. There were a lot of people drowned. Some were never found."

"Why was that, Ma?"

"It runs from Dublin right down into Wexford and into the sea. The depths vary and there could be whirlpools too!"

"Don't worry, Ma. Dan is going to teach me to swim. He taught Miley and he can swim like a fish!"

CHAPTER THREE

It took him two days to make the rod. He was always going up and down to the campsite to see Miley.

"Has your Mother got any mustard?"

"I don't know, but I will ask her"

"Make sure it's the powder stuff."

"What do you want that for?"

"We will need plenty of worms for bait."

Mary gave him some mustard next day and he took it up to Miley.

"Pick up that old bean tin and give it a wash."

He got an empty milk bottle and filled it with water. Then he mixed the mustard through the water.

"We're ready now. Let's go to the football field."

When they reached the field, they went up around the hard ground beside the goalposts.

"See all those wormholes? Well, pour the mix down those holes."

In no time the can was full.

"What does the mustard do?" asked Michael.

"It scalds the worms out of the hole. That's how you get plenty of worms."

"Right, we will go fishing tomorrow afternoon. Call up before one and we will fish at the weir."

The next day, Michael and Lassie appeared and they walked up towards the weir.

"What have you in the bag?"

"Mam made up some sandwiches and minerals for us."

"Your Mother is a Saint. She's the nicest woman I have ever met."

"Yeah," replied Michael, "She likes you, Miley."

"And I am very fond of her. Let's try and catch her a few trout."

Miley showed him how to put on a worm on a hook. They had great fun. After a while Michael pulled in a lovely trout. It was not long till he pulled in another fine trout.

"It really is your lucky day. You must have said a few prayers last night," suggested Miley.

"It's not my day at all. Are you putting something special on those worms?" asked Miley.

"Not at all, it's beginners luck".

They packed it in after a while and went back to the campsite.

"Look, Dan, what do you think?"

"Holy God, you must have caught the grandfathers of the trout. They're so big, the biggest I've seen yet."

Michael was so excited as he walked home with Lassie behind him. He ran in the door. "Look, Ma! These are for our supper."

"They're the finest trout I have ever seen."

"Dan said the same, Ma. He said I caught their Grandfathers and their great grandfathers."

Even when his Father came home he was delighted.

"You really are a great little man."

He felt so proud of himself that night as he kissed his mother before he went to bed.

"I love you, Ma"

"And you, Son."

Over the next week Dan had Michael swimming like a fish. He would tie a rope around him and tell him to jump into the barrow. He wasn't scared, as he knew he had a tight hold on the rope. They only had a week left of their holidays and he was going to enjoy it.

The next day when he got there, Dan asked how his Mother enjoyed the fish.

"She is cooking them tonight."

"Are you going fishing today?"

"No, Dad, we are taking Lassie for a good walk."

"Did you hear that, girl? They're taking you for a long walk."

She started barking. They walked miles up the riverbank and got over a fence that led them to a big stream. It was a very warm day and the hot sun was draining their energy.

"Let's sit down for a while, I am tired" said Michael.

They lay down beside the stream and they could hear Lassie getting a drink.

"Look at all those trout going up the stream."

"Yes, it runs into the Barrow further down."

"Patrick is starting in the Christian brother's school next week."

"I don't fancy that school after what my Dad told me."

"What did he tell you?"

"He was reared in one of those industrial schools when his Parents died. He was ten years old. He told me that it was a living nightmare that they used to beat the shit out of him for nothing at all. He was in there till he was sixteen years old and he said it was only a torture chamber. That is the reason he does not want me getting into trouble, they would send you there for the least thing. A lot of the boys that were there only missed schools a few days, or robbed something. My Father had an Aunt who could not look after him, so they sent him there. He told me that through the night you could hear other boys crying, after been whipped naked."

"Jesus, it must have been very bad there."

"Well, I hope they never send me there."

"Me neither."

"I am going for a swim to cool myself down."

"But we have no swimming trunks"

"That doesn't matter," said Miley as he stripped naked on the bank.

He jumped in.

"Someone will see you, Miley."

"Ah, no one comes around here; it's lovely, come on in."

Michael got up and stripped naked as well and jumped in.

"It is lovely and cool."

Lassie was barking like mad on the bank.

"Come on girl, jump in."

And she did. They had great fun with Lassie in the water and after a while got out and lay on the bank. The sun dried them off, until Lassie came beside them and started shaking herself off. She drowned the boys.

"Oh, Lassie, go away."

They lay down again until they were dry.

"We better move. Ma will have something to eat."

So they got dressed and walked back towards the camp. When they got near the camp they heard singing so they sneaked behind a bush and listened. Maggie was singing and she had a beautiful voice, what is that song she is singing' 'The whistling Gypsy'.

"It is a beautiful song and your Mother sings it so well. Can you get me the words of that song?"

"I will."

When she finished they came out.

"Did you have a good times boys?"

"Yes, Maggie, we did."

"You are a lovely singer!"

"Go away, Michael, sure there are better singers than me."

"But not as beautiful."

"Come on now, you little charmer and have a bite to eat. You must be hungry. I have a bit left by for Lassie."

Dan was busy making milk cans and Maggie was making flowers out of shavings. He watched Maggie put different colored dyes on the shavings and leave them for drying. She got lengths of thin wire and then tied in some different colored shavings. When she was finished she had the most beautiful artificial flowers you could ever have set your eyes on.

"What do you do with all the milk cans and the flowers, Dan?"

"Maggie and myself sell them. We travel around most of the villages and people buy them."

"That's great."

The school opened in September but Michael hated the thoughts of going back. This summer was the best he ever experienced. When he got home, he'd have his dinner and then sit down and listen to the radio. He would only see Miley in school or at the weekends but he missed him a lot when the weather was good. He liked Maureen Potter but nothing could beat Jimmy Clitroe, he'd have him in stitches. Some nights he would listen to Dingo and take the floor. It was dancing music but he liked his voice. Patrick would be always studying in his room or serving Mass. He was busy all the time. Mary was out one frosty day while Michael was at home by himself. Patrick came home crying.

"What's wrong with you?" asked Michael.

"My feet are freezing in these wellies."

"I'll warm them up for you."

Michael had a plan. Off he went into the kitchen

and got a kettle of boiling water. He poured it down his Brother's boot.

"Ah! You fucking fool, you roasted the foot off me," cried Patrick while jumping in agony. Seamus came in and was shocked to see what had happened. He beat Michael black and blue with a sally rod and threw him into bed. When his Mother came home she had to get Doctor Byrne for Patrick. He put some ointment on the burn to sooth it and some gauze and dressing to protect it. The Doctor advised Mary to keep Patrick off school for at least a week and to reapply the dressing and ointment herself.

Patrick told his mother that he'd have to serve early Mass the next morning but his Father assured him that he would let Father O'Leary know.

"And then I will call in on Brother Burke and tell him too. I have to go up and see Joe, so I will be passing that way."

When Seamus went out, Mary took some food to Michael.

"What were you thinking of Son? He cannot go to school for a week now."

"I was only trying to warm him up, Mam"

"Well, you certainly done that. You roasted the foot off him!"

"He said a curse too, Ma, and I never heard him cursing before"

"Why, what did he say?"

"He called me a fucking fool, Ma. I'm not a fool Ma, am I?"

"No, you are not. You're a clever boy."

"I will always love you, Ma, even when I grow up!"

"And you will always be my baby and you are not stupid. Good night," she said as she bent over to kiss him.

It was two weeks before Patrick could attend school and in the meantime the new Curate had arrived. His name was Father Tony Walsh. He looked like a young Priest. When he met Patrick both of them got on very well.

"Father O' Leary thinks the world of you. He was telling me that you were a great worker for the Parish. Did you ever think of joining the church?"

"I have thought about many times. That's why I am saving up. You need plenty of money."

"Not now, as the church pays for your education. But then you have to go wherever they send you. If you had money like my Parents had, you can stay in your own country. I have an Uncle who is a Bishop."

"I wouldn't mind where they sent me."

"Well, I believe they are sent all over the world."

"I'd like that."

"Well, when you have decided, let me know and we'll have another talk."

"Don't worry, I will. I think it is something that is my vocation for life."

"Well, I hope you're right."

Halloween was fast approaching so Michael and Miley decided to get a head start. They were going over to the woods and they took Lassie with them. They were going to pick some hazelnuts. When they arrived, the trees were abundant with nuts. Michael couldn't believe the amount of nuts that were there.

"We'll take off our jumpers, we'll get more that way."

"The Squirrels must be all dead. They take most of them for the winter."

"Or maybe they were too shagging lazy to collect them."

"Where are we going to get a mask for Halloween?" asked Miley.

"Well," replied Michael, "I am going to ask that Midwife for a loan of her face. She would frighten you in daylight, never mind the dark!"

They both started to laugh.

"Michael, did you ever see a Squirrel swimming?"

"No, never."

"Well, you know that they always swim on their back."

"You're joking me, Miley."

"No, I'm not."

"But why would they swim on their backs?"

"To keep their nuts dry, you fool."

Michael pissed himself laughing.

"I must tell that one to my Mother when I go home, that was good."

They left the woods and went back to the camp-fire.

"Look at all the nuts we got!"

"Holy God, boys, you must have cleaned out the trees. Did you leave any for the poor Squirrels?"

"They're all right, sure they sleep through the winter, and they won't need nuts."

Dan was busy cutting out the middle of two heads of beet. When he was finished he cut out two eyes, a nose and a mouth. Then he stuck a candle into each of the heads of beet. When it got dark, he lit them.

"There you are, boys, put them up in a dark spot and they will frighten anyone."

During Halloween night, the two boys went to Murphy's field and lit a bit of a fire. They told each other ghost stories. Miley was shitting himself when he had to go home. It was a good job his Father came to collect him. The week before Christmas they went back into the woods again, this time for holly and a tree. Lassie took out after a rabbit and caught him as he entered the burrow.

"Good girl," said Miley, encouraging her.

Miley took the rabbit, as his mother would make a pot of stew out of it. They went back for the holly and the tree and Miley gave Michael a hand to carry the stuff home.

"I will see you tomorrow, Miley," Michael said as he started to carry the tree and holly indoors.

Over the week Michael helped to decorate the house and the Christmas tree. Patrick came in and told his Mother and Father that he had to serve midnight Mass on Christmas Eve.

"We all might as well go to that Mass, as we will have to collect Patrick anyway," suggested Seamus.

So it was agreed and they all ended up going to midnight Mass. They all stood outside the church admiring the huge crib. The boys from the Brother's school had put it up. When Mass was over, they had to wait for a few minutes until Patrick got dressed. He walked out with Father Tony and Patrick introduced him to his family.

"You have a great boy here, you should be proud of him. He does wonders for this church."

"Father, we are very proud. He's such a gentle child and very quiet, not like this lad here."

"He's only young. Give him time to prove himself. Well, I will say goodnight to you all. Have a very happy Christmas and a peaceful New Year."

"Thank you, Father and a very happy Christmas to yourself and Father O'Leary."

They walked home through the village together and when they got to their cottage Mary made them all something to eat. After the meal their mother suggested that they go to bed as Santa Claus would be there shortly.

"But Dad, he is here already. You're Santa!"

"Who told you that?"

"We knew from last year, Dad. Sure, we watched you putting the presents under the tree. You did not notice us because you were stone drunk. You nearly brought down the Christmas tree with you."

"Was I drunk last year, Mary?"

"Of course you were. This is the only year I have seen you sober."

"Well, I am going to start now because I don't have to get up in the morning."

"Good night, Ma, goodnight Da and a very happy Christmas to you's."

"Goodnight, boys and many happy returns."

Mary was up early and had the breakfast ready.

She was expecting Joe and Sally there any minute. It wasn't long till they arrived.

"Where are they all, still in the bed?"

"Joe, sit down there and have a bite to eat."

"We have news. We wanted to let you and Seamus know first."

"Well? Don't keep me in suspense."

"Should we tell her, Sally?"

"Tell me what?"

"She's pregnant."

"At long last! Are you sure?"

"Yes, Mary, the Doctor confirmed it."

"Oh, I am so happy for you, for both of you. Congratulations."

"Thank you and don't forget I will be there for you, to help you along."

"I just can't wait, I'm overjoyed."

Seamus came down and heard the news.

"And there was me thinking that you had no lead in your pencil."

"I was starting to think that myself, Seamus, but I must have got a bit somewhere."

"Well, I am glad for you Joe and you, Sally. It must be the best news since you were married. This is going to be the best Christmas we will ever have. I will make sure of that," said Seamus.

"When are you due, Sally?" asked Mary.

"The worst time of all, August, it'll be so warm. I dread that Midwife coming. She scares me."

"You will find out that she has a great heart behind that mask."

They all had a brilliant Christmas and when the boys heard that Sally was pregnant they too were happy for them.

Michael's confirmation was coming up soon and a trip to Dublin was planned. Mary brought him in for his dinner and he asked her if she had any money to spare.

"What do you want the money for?"

"Well, Ma, I would like to buy Dan a belt. He always has that twine"

"Well, if it is for Dan, sure, we will have a look around and see can we pick him up a nice one!"

"With a horses head on the buckle, Ma!"

"Of course, whatever you say."

They went around a lot of shops before they found the right one.

"He will like that one, Ma!"

The girl wrapped it up for him and his Mother suggested that they brought home some Dublin rock as well.

"It's very sweet and sticky, Ma."

"Not for you. What about Maggie and Miley?"

"I forgot about them."

"Oh Ma, it's a good job you came. You always think of the poor. We are both alike."

"And your Father and Brother are the same as well. They're both alike."

"Yes, Ma, you can say that again! They would not swap their shit for currant cakes."

She started laughing at the way he expressed himself. When they got back, his Mother reminded him of the Brother's School.

"You will be going there after the holidays."

"I don't fancy going there but I have to anyway."

"I was told that they're baskets. They beat you for nothing."

"Less of the language. Patrick seems to like them."

"They don't hit him. They aren't going to hit a saint now, are they, Ma?"

"I suppose you are right. Just try to be good."

"I bet you any money that Patrick becomes a Priest, Mam."

"You're joking me! Did he say that to you?"

"No, but I can smell it!"

"God, you must have a great nose."

"You're Father is hoping that he will go into the mill with him."

"Don't count on it. I bet you I'm right."

"Well, we'll just have to wait and see who's right or wrong."

Michael was getting confirmed that Sunday. He got up early that Saturday and went up to the camp. Lassie was with him and she ran on ahead.

"Look at that, Maggie! Michael is on the way. Come here, girl."

Lassie went straight to Dan.

"Hello, Maggie. Where's Miley?"

"He's gone to get a churn of water. He has to have a bath for his confirmation tomorrow. It will be your last big day until you both get married."

"We won't get married! Sure, it's a fool's game!"

"Wait till you get older. You'll change your mind."

"Here, Maggie. Some Dublin rock for you and Miley."

"You are a grand lad. You always think of us."

"I have a present for you too, Dan," Michael said, handing him the parcel.

"God, what's this?"

"Open it."

When he opened it his eyes lit up. When he saw the belt a tear ran down his cheek. "Look, Maggie. It's the first present I got in years and something I needed badly."

"Well, do you like it, Dan?"

"Yes, of course. It will be my pride and joy. Oh, you are like a Son to me."

They heard the pony coming. Lassie started barking.

"Here comes Miley now."

"Hello, Michael."

"Come here, Son and see what he got me in Dublin. Ah, its grand and it has a horses head and all. Thank you, Michael, from the bottom of my heart."

"Well, you can throw away that bit of twine now."

"Here's some rock for you, son, he always comes back with something for us. I did not think you would be up today on account of our Confirmation tomorrow."

"I had to come up to give you your rock and give Dan the belt I got him."

Maggie put the kettle on.

"Pour out Michael a cup of tea and see if there is a bit of rabbit for my girl in there," said Dan.

Lassie started to bark at Dan.

"Sometimes I think that you know everything I say."

Miley walked back to the start of the village with Michael.

"Goodbye, I will see you tomorrow in the church."

"Yes, we will have a good day. Don't forget to put on your best suit!"

"I will. The Nuns gave me one."

Both of the boys got their confirmation that Sunday. The church was full. Michael was wearing long trousers with a lovely blue blazer, a white shirt and a blue tie. He met Miley and gave him a few shillings.

"You can get a few pints on me" joked Michael.

"Yes," replied Miley, "Pints of water."

"Miley, you look great in them clothes, no wonder the Midwife is looking. She fancies you."

"Will you ever feck off! Sure, your Lassie's arse is better looking than her."

Mary went over to him.

"Oh Miley, you look so handsome. That suit looks a treat on you."

"Thanks, Mrs. Flynn."

"Here, get something nice," she said handing him five shillings.

"Oh thank you very much," said Miley looking shocked.

"And tell your Mam and Dad I was asking for them."

"I will to be sure, Mam. They will be waiting for me outside."

"Well, we will be going. The men want to go for a drink. It's too late for us to go anywhere else."

Mary told Michael that she would bring him somewhere the next week. They went back to the cottage and Michael got changed. He then decided to go up to the camp and he took Lassie with him. Maggie and Dan were having a beer around the fire when they arrived.

"Ah, here's our favorite lad, come and sit with us. Will you have a drink Son?"

"No I don't drink, but I'll have a slug of it. God, Dan, that's great stuff."

"What are we going to do now Miley?" asked Michael.

"Get Mam to sing. Go on, Maggie, sing the whistling gypsy!"

"Anything for you, son."

She started to sing. It was beautiful and they all joined in. Even Lassie started to howl.

"Come here me old girl," said Dan.

Lassie went over to him.

"I think there's a bit of a human in you. You're the smartest dog that I've ever seen. What school did you go to?" laughed Dan. "I hope it wasn't the Christian Brothers. They're a shower of baskets. Excuse my French, boys!"

"If we tell him tomorrow that he was talking to the Dog, he won't believe us," said Miley.

"He's pissed and look at your Mother, she's falling asleep. Well, I better be going. Come on, Lassie."

"I will see you tomorrow."

"Good luck."

Chapter Four

They were off for the summer now and Michael loved that there was no school till September.

He got up early the next morning. His Mother and Brother were sitting at the table.

"I'm taking Michael to Bray on Friday for the day. Are you coming with us?"

"I can't go, Ma. They're cleaning out the graveyard on Friday. I promised Father Tony that I would help."

"What do you want to clean out the graveyard for?" asked Michael.

"To keep it nice and tidy."

"That's stupid. I'd prefer to go to Bray."

"Well, would you like to rest in a dirty grave-yard?"

"Sure, feck it. How would it matter? You'd be dead anyway," replied Michael.

"Have you any respect for anyone, to say a thing like that?"

"Well, if you're in a coffin, how the feck would you know if it was clean or not?" "Less of the swearing, Son!"

"I am sorry, Ma, but he gives me the pips."

"I bet if Father Tony was going to Bray, you'd be holding his hand."

"I am away, Ma. I'm not listening to any more of this."

"See you later, Son."

"Patrick, before you go, will you do me a favor?"

"What's that?"

"Would you kiss me arse and tell me the flavor?"

"You are heading for hell!"

"No," said Michael, I'm not. I am heading to Bray, without you."

"Thank God. I hope you drown there, at least I'd be rid of you."

"No fear of that happening, I can swim!"

"You can only swim in bed, when you piss yourself."

Patrick went out the door like a mad man.

"Michael, you shouldn't say things like that to your Brother. Listen, why don't you ask Miley to join us? Sure he never gets to go anywhere."

"That'd be great, Ma. I'll go up and ask him now."

"Well, keep it between ourselves, we don't want anyone to know, especially your Dad."

Off he and Lassie went, up to camp. He met Miley on his way up.

"I'm going to the village to get some milk," said Miley.

"I'll walk back with you, Jimmy Griffin's is the nearest."

"I have two pence. We can get some liquorices balls."

"By the way, we're going to Bray on Friday and Mam would like you to come."

"That's fantastic, I'd love to go."

"At least we'd get away from here for the day."

When they reached the shop, Miley bought the milk and Michael asked for the sweets. Jimmy counted them out and put them into a paper bag.

"What's this?" asked Michael. "You only gave me sixteen balls for two pence. Pat Carpenter gives me two dozen."

"Well, let me tell you, young man. My balls are a lot bigger than Pat Carpenters!" When they went out the door, Michael said, "No wonder, he went to the same school as my Dad. They're both tight fisted. A spanner wouldn't get the money out of their hands."

When they reached the camp Maggie had the kettle boiling.

"Sit down there now boys and I will make you's a grand cup of tea."

"How is your head, Maggie? You were in a right state last night. Where's Dan?"

"He's only getting up now. He kept me awake all night snoring."

"You were snoring yourself, Ma. I could hear the two of you from the tent."

"I don't snore, Miley. It was your Dad that you heard."

"Aye and cows don't eat grass."

Dan came out holding onto his head.

"Is your head sore? Lassie wants to have a chat with you," jeered Michael.

"Sure, any fool knows that dogs can't talk."

"Well, you were talking to her last night."

"Oh, I may give up the drink. Could you tell me if she answered back?"

"Well, she was doing a lot of barking at you," said Michael.

"And I don't remember a thing."

"Dan, Mam wants to know if we can take Miley to Bray on Friday."

"I don't mind at all Son, but watch it, all the young

girls will be around this weather." "That'd be grand," said Michael, "We might bring back a couple."

"Oh, leave them where they are until you get older. Sometimes they're a pain in the ass."

Friday was long awaited and finally it arrived. Miley said goodbye to his parents and headed off.

"Have a good day, Son. You can tell us all about it when you get back."

When they got there, Mary took them both to have their photographs taken.

"This is great, Mrs. Flynn. My Parents never had a photo of me."

"Well, when they arrive I'll send a few up to you. You's both looked like real little angels. Come on now and we'll get something to eat then we'll go over to the carnival." When they finished eating, they had a marvelous time on the bumper cars.

"Would you's like to go on the ghost train? It might frighten you's though."

"Not if we don't see the Midwife," said Michael.

"God, you give that woman an awful time."

They got on the ghost train and had a great laugh.

"Look at that, Miley, there's the skeleton."

"It's the Midwife having a bath."

Mary could only laugh at them, she was enjoying

it herself. They took a walk down the beach. It was packed.

"Did ye bring your trunks?"

"Of course, Ma. We're going in for a swim. Where can we change?"

"Do you see that building over there? Go in the side door."

They came out and she watched them go into the water. When they came back out, she had two towels spread out on the sand.

"I'm going for a bit of a walk. Will you two be all right here till I get back?"

"Of course, Ma. Sure, we are not babies anymore."

"All right then. See you's later."

They were laying face down soaking up the sun when they heard a girl's voice.

"Would you's have a cigarette on you by any chance?"

When they turned over, there were two lovely looking girls looking down on them. "Sorry we don't smoke."

Both of them were wearing bathing costumes.

"Well, what are you's up to?" asked the girls.

"We're only here for the day. Mam took us here cos we have just made our confirmation"

"Where are you's from?"

"Mount Leinster."

"Where the fuck is that?"

"It's about ten miles outside Carlow."

"We've never heard tell of it."

"Where are you two from?" asked Michael.

"We're on holidays here from London, we both live in a place called Cricklewood."

"We're staying in Dublin with our cousins."

"I was there a few times. It's not a bad place. Plenty of shops up there." said Michael.

"You should see our country sometime. It's not as great as people say it is"

"Well, why did you come over here then?"

"To see our Grandparents. Only for that we would have stayed at home."

"What are your names anyway?" I'm Michael Flynn and this is my friend Miley O'Brien."

"Well I'm Ann Fitzgerald and she's Rosie Carr. Would you two like to join us in a swim?"

"Why not, it's too warm lying here."

They had a great time in the water with the girls, and after they went to a secluded spot. They started messing about and Ann gave Michael a kiss.

"Wow, that was grand. Gimme another one".

Miley was kissing Rosie. They messed about for another while and then girls had to go. The four of them walked back to the beach together.

"If you ever come to London, don't forget to look us up."

"We'll be seeing you, goodbye."

"You never gave us your address," Michael shouted after them, but they were gone.

Mary had seen them coming back and was wondering who the two girls were. She waited till they were going back home on the bus to ask them.

"I saw you with two good looking girls on the beach today. Did you enjoy yourselves?"

"Yes, Ma, they were from London. They're staying with their cousin in Dublin."

"Had you a good day, Miley?"

"It was the best day I had in my life, thanks to you."

"Here's a little souvenir from Bray. You can give it to your parents."

"Thank you very much."

Dan was waiting for Miley when he got off the bus as it was very late.

"Did you have a good time lads?"

"Yes, Dad. It was great!"

"Thank you, Mam, for your kindness."

"He deserved a break, Dan."

"Well, we will be seeing you. Safe home now."

"Thank you again, Mrs. Flynn, as long as I live I will never forget this day" said Miley.

"Good night."

They were tired when they got in and Michael said goodnight to his Mother.

"Good night, son."

"Thanks for the good day, Mam. I love you always."

When he had his breakfast next morning he left with Lassie and went up to Dan's. "Well I heard that you had a great time yesterday. Thank your Mother for the souvenir."

"Where is Miley?"

"He's still asleep. He was tired out after your trip."

"Go in there and give him a shout or he will never get up."

He entered the tent. Miley was still asleep so he tapped him on the face.

"God, Michael, what time of the day is it?"

"You're late, it's a quarter to eleven."

"I have to get up and go fill the milk churn with fresh water."

"Hurry up then. I will go with you and give you a hand."

They had a cup of tea and then got the pony and trap ready and threw up the churn. They travelled to the nearest water pump; it was a half a mile away. When they had the churn full Miley let Michael take the reins.

"This is great, you have a wonderful life. I should have been a traveller."

"We would never have seen Bray then and them two lovely girls."

When they got the water back, Dan gave them a hand to unload it.

"We are off to the village, Dad, to have a look around."

"All right, Son."

When they got to the village, they watched Paraffin Joe going to the cottages. He had an ass and cart with a barrel of paraffin and some measuring cans.

"Look who is giving him a hand, it's Dixie."

"He's simple and is in my brother's class."

"Come on and we will follow them."

So they walked behind them. Michael knew that Joe would stay in one of the cottages to have a cup of tea. Dixie would go on selling the paraffin so when they got near the midwife's cottage. Michael got talking to him.

"Do you like going to the Brother's school?"

"God, lads, what ever you do, stay away from there, they're cruel gets."

"But we're going after the holidays. My Brother knows you well."

"What's his name?"

"Patrick Flynn."

"Sure, he's a great friend of mine and you're his little Brother. You will be with me in school as there's three of us kept back this year."

"That's great. Sure, we can be the best of friends."

"Would you like that?"

"I sure would. I don't have a lot of friends."

"Can I give you a hand for a few minutes?"

"Aye, but watch the boss coming."

"I have to go in here to the Midwife. You can fill that gallon measure for me."

Michael knew that there was a water pump a few yards away.

"Hurry up, fill the measure with water."

Dixie came out with the glass bowl off the Midwife's cooker, took off the top and filled it.

"God, Dixie, it holds exactly a gallon. Oh, here's your boss coming, see you at school. We will be off!"

"Thanks for the little help. Sure, I will see you again."

The lads went off laughing their hearts out.

"She'll do no cooking tonight."

They were on their way into Jamie Griffins shop when they noticed an ad in the window. Fruit pickers wanted urgently, apply to Manor farm.

"That's just outside the village."

"Let's go and see if we can get a job for the summer."

"We could save a lot of money."

It only took them twenty minutes to get there. They talked to the Farmer.

"Well boys, if you are here by nine in the morning, you can start."

"Thank you, Sir."

They went home and told their Mothers.

"Well, it will keep you out of trouble."

Miley was waiting outside the village for Michael to arrive. It was early. He saw him coming, holding a bag full of stuff.

"What's in the bag?"

"It is our food for the break times. Mam made up some for you as well."

They started picking strawberries and when their boxes were full they checked them in.

"Are you working together?" the Checker asked.

"Yes, we are."

"Well, your number will be four so each time you come up just give that number."

They had their break and the farmer had the water boiling for them to make tea. There was a good crowd of boys and girls picking the fruit and the lads loved it. They made twelve shillings between them for their first day. That was good.

On their way home, they bumped into Dixie.

"How are you?"

"We are working now."

"I lost my job over that stupid Midwife. She told the boss that I sold her water. She said that I ruined her cooker so he had to go and buy her a new one."

"And did he give you any money?"

"All I got was a slap in the face from him."

"God, that's bad. Would you like to come and pick fruit with us?"

"I would love to! Would I make much money?"

"It all depends on what you pick."

"I'd be good at that. What time do you start?"

"Meet us at Jimmy's shop at half eight."

"All right then. Can I take some fruit home?"

"I don't think he would mind. The only thing, Dixie, is you have to tell the Checker that your number is four because you'll be with us. Will you think of that number?"

"Yes. Right lads, I'll see you in the morning."

"Good luck, Dixie.

"We will make plenty of money now he could be a great picker."

"But what happens when they are paying us at the end of the week?"

"That's easy, we'll work for him for one day and he'll work four for us."

They all met the next morning and Dixie was delighted to have some work. He was a good worker and every time he went up with the lads it was number four. On the way home Michael asked him if he liked his job.

"Yes, it's great!"

They saw Joe's ass and cart tied up at one of the cottages with a barrel on the back. "Look Dixie, he must be in there having his tea. He's always in that house, the mean git."

As they were passing, Michael turned on the tap and the oil was flowing down the village. Dixie was laughing his heart out.

"Now," said Michael. "You got your own back on him."

"See you in the morning; I'll be at the shop."

"Right, Dixie. Good luck."

When the last day of the week came, Michael told him to change his number. So when they brought up the fruit, Michael told the Checker to give Dixie a new number. So now he was number twelve and the three of them worked all day on that number. They got paid that night and the lads had a good wage between them.

"How much did you get, Dixie?"

"I only got ten bob for the week."

"They must have taxed you but you will get it all back when you finish."

"That's all right then. Sure, they are only saving it for me."

"We are picking raspberries next week and they pay you by weight."

The following week Dixie gave the bucket of raspberries to Michael to check in.

"He's a nice lad. See the way he carries the two buckets up to give us a rest!"

"A grand lad," said Dixie. "Sure, there's not too many lads like Michael."

Dixie went to the far side of the hedge to pick and came back in a panic.

"What's wrong with you?"

"There's a girl in there pissing in a bucket of raspberries."

The lads went around there like a rocket and saw the girl still at it.

"It makes the buckets weight heavier. You get a few extra pounds. You won't tell, will you?"

"Let us have a look and we won't tell."

So she lifted her frock to let the boys see her do it.

"Holy Mother, so that's the difference between a boy and a girl!" said Michael astonished.

"How do you hold your piss standing up?"

"It's the way that girls are made."

They went back over to Dixie.

"God you were right, she was pissing in the bucket."

"I told you so, she's a dirty bitch! I will never eat raspberry jam again."

"She told us that it makes the bucket weigh heavier and you get extra money for it."

"God, if that is true I'm going to do the same!" said Dixie.

So he takes it out and pisses in the bucket.

"You may take up the bucket, Michael, in case they smell the piss."

"No problem!"

It was Friday afternoon and they all would be getting paid that night, which was great. Michael saw 'Dirty Eye' coming up on the other side of the hedge. He was the Foreman.

"I will check this bucket in and see what happens."

They pushed their luck. Dixie was feeling like another piss and decided to use a second bucket. He didn't see the Foreman behind the hedge.

"You dirty little fecker! Get out of here, you're sacked!"

He wouldn't give him a chance so that was the end of Dixie's fruit picking. On the way home the lads met Dixie who was waiting for his wages.

81

"He would not pay you! Why?"

"He said he had to throw out the full barrel of raspberries over you pissing in them."

"My mother is going to kill me when I get home!"

"Here's two pounds, Dixie. That's all we can afford to give you."

"Thanks, Michael. You're the best friend I ever met."

"Sure, I'll see you in school."

The lads worked until they made enough money. Then they finished up the fruit picking for the summer.

"We still have two weeks to ourselves before we start in the brothers, so let's enjoy it."

CHAPTER FIVE

Maggie and Dan were delighted thanks to Miley as he gave most of his money to them. Michael's Mother wouldn't take a penny off him.

"Keep it, Son. You earned it."

Dan promised Miley a good night; it was to take place that Saturday.

"Could you come up and stay for the night, Michael? Sure, we can sleep in the tent."

"I'll have to ask my Mother. I know that my Father wouldn't allow me. I will let you know tomorrow when I call up. I better be going. Come on, Lassie."

When he asked his Mother, she agreed but warned him not to let his Father know.

"But he'll miss me if I am not in the house. How am I going to answer that?"

"I will tell him that you have been invited to a birthday party and I'll say that his Mother asked me if you could stay the night."

He went up and told Miley that he could stay the night.

"That's great. We'll have a great old laugh."

"What are we going to do today?"

"We might as well go for a swim or a walk."

"Right. Sure, we can do both."

They got up and headed up the track.

"I feel sorry for making a fool out of Dixie."

"Sure, he made us a good few bob. Anyway, it was a good laugh. He still thinks that we are his best friends."

"Well, we might as well be as he might come in handy again."

When they reached the stream, they lay down on the bank as the heat got to them.

"That girl that pissed in the bucket of raspberries, I wonder will she show us again?"

"That was the first time that I ever seen between a girl's legs."

"Ah, we should have told Dixie."

"We should have called him to come around the hedge. We would have got a good laugh out of him."

"She wasn't bad looking either but not as good looking as the two we met in Bray."

"I dreamt of them every night since I came back. They were beautiful."

"Did you get randy?"

"Nearly every night. I had a wet dream about them."

"The same as that. Sure, there is nothing as good as a hand shandy."

"I wonder if Dixie knows what a hand shandy is?"

"We must ask him for the craic."

"Come on, I'm getting in for a swim to cool down. It is getting to warm."

They stripped and Michael started to laugh.

"You're randy! Thinking about them girls, aren't you?"

"Why do think I am going in for a swim?"

"I want to drown him, to keep him cool."

When they got out, they sat down on the bank and let the sun dry them off.

"We better go while we are cooled down; it's a good walk back!"

Lassie jumped into the barrow on the way back after two young Swans.

"Come out of there, leave the baby swans alone. You're a daft Dog!"

She swam back out and the boys ran before she shook herself off.

Dan was making his milk cans while Maggie made the lads something to eat.

"We're going into the village for a look around, we'll see you later."

They had a few bob so they went into the shop and bought some sweets, minerals and crisps.

"Let's go to Murphy's field and we can sit down there for a while and eat." They sat down in their usual place and whom did they see? Only poor auld Dixie.

"What are you doing around here?"

"I'm collecting a few sticks for my auld one."

"Sit down there. Miley, give him a drink out of that bag."

"Here's some crisps as well."

"They took my Father away to the loony farm last night and my Ma is tearing her hair out. I had to get out she is in bad form. I wanted to go with my Father but they wouldn't let me go. My Ma said that I'd be there soon enough."

"You mean to tell me that you want to go into the mental hospital? Are you mad or what?"

"Well, my Ma said it was a loony farm. I only wanted to go and see the animals."

"It is not a farm, that's only a nickname they put on the place. It's a mad house. They keep you there until you die. You come back out of there in a coffin."

"And what would you be doing all day in those places?" asked Dixie.

"You'd be sitting on your arse all day talking to yourself; eating, shitting and pissing."

"Michael, ask him about the hand shandy."

"Did you ever have a hand shandy Dixie?"

"A few times a year, mostly around the Christmas."

"Were they good for you?"

"My Dad was better than me at the hand shandy. He grew up at it. The only thing you need plenty of Guinness and bottles of lemonade. They laughed their hearts out.

"God, Dixie! You're a right character. You're mad! When you went into the midwife's house, did you see her talking bird?"

"What are you saying, Michael? Sure, there's no such thing as a talking bird."

"Well, everyone around the village says she has one. She was supposed to have brought it back from London."

"She wouldn't let me inside her door but I didn't hear anyone talking."

"Well, some night we are going to find out."

"Yes," agreed Miley. "We'll wait for the dark evenings."

"Come on, Miley, we better be going. See you later, Dixie."

"Can I go with you when you are going to see the talking bird?"

"Of course you can."

Saturday night came and Michael went up to the campsite, followed by Lassie in tow. Dan had a load of drink bought along with minerals and sweets and a good fire going.

"Sit down there Son and take out a mineral and some sweets out of that bag. Come here girl, I've something for you too."

He took out a big bone with plenty of meat on it. She came over to him and started licking him.

"Hold on, girl! I had a wash this morning."

"Ma, will you tell Michael his fortune tonight?"

"He'd have to cross my palm with silver."

"Would a sixpenny piece do, Maggie? It's the only bit of silver on me."

"Of course it will. Come over here and I will see what the future holds for you." Maggie took his hand.

"Now cross my palm with silver and behold the future. I see a dark cloud hanging over you Son.. There's plenty of trouble on the way. Michael, promise me one thing."

"I will, Maggie."

"Get yourself a holy medal - it'll keep you safe."

"Ah, don't mind her, Son. She's trying to frighten the shit out of you," said Dan.

"I am not. I just want you to be careful. There is some danger ahead for you. Now I have to throw this sixpence away."

So she threw it over her head and into the darkness.

"Michael, she'll pick up that sixpence tomorrow when it gets bright," laughed Dan.

"I will not, Dan O'Brien. That'd cast an evil spell on him. I've already seen that dark cloud."

"Ah, don't worry, Maggie. Sure my brother has plenty of Lourdes medals," assured Michael.

"Well, you make sure and get one to put around your neck for luck."

When they got fairly drunk, Dan offered Miley a bottle of Guinness.

"Can I have one as well, Dan? I am sick of drinking minerals."

"Ah, drink away, boys. Sure, a drop of beer won't harm you at all."

So the two boys started drinking and before the night was over they too were singing. They were drunk getting into the tent and Miley brought the oil lamp in with him.

"Whatever you do don't hit off that lamp or we both will be cremated in the morning."

They stripped down and the two of them fell into a heap on the mattress. When they woke up the next morning, both of them had very sore heads.

"God, I will never drink that stuff again."

"I don't know how your Mam and Dad drink it."

Dan and Maggie were up having the tea when the lads came out of the tent. "God, you both look like two boiled shites. What you need is a strong cup of tea."

"Dan, how the hell can you drink that stuff? Sure me head is bursting with a headache."

"That's what Arthur does for you, he gets the money and we get the headaches. You'll get used to it. It's good for the body."

In the mean time Sally and Joe had a new baby girl and they were all delighted. Father O'Leary christened the baby. It was Patrick and his Mother who stood for the child. They went back to their cottage for a party. It was great. They called her Emma. She was a beautiful looking child.

They started in the Brother's school the next September. Michael was going to miss taking Lassie for her walk up to Dan's. The weekends would be the only time now that he could go to the camp.

Their first day at school was a disaster. When they were in the schoolyard at playtime, two lads came up to them and started calling Miley a tinker. A row developed. Dixie was there telling the lads that they were his friends and not to fight them.

"Why are you fond of the tinkers as well?" asked David.

"Just stay out of this, we'll settle it" said Michael.

The boy's hit them and Brother Burke came on the scene and caned the four of them. After school they started fighting again. Michael told the two lads to meet them on Saturday afternoon to finish it.

"Right, said one of the lads, name your place."

"Murphy's field at two o'clock."

"We'll meet you there."

When Saturday came, Michael and Miley were waiting in the field but there was no sign of the other boys.

"They have chickened out. We'll give them five more minutes." Said Michael.

They were just about to go when they saw them arrive with Dixie.

"You're late. You must have had second thoughts."

"Well, we're here now."

Michael and Miley beat the shit out of them.

"We have had enough. Leave it at that." Said one of the boys.

"I told you that they were two hardy snipes. You wouldn't listen, you gobshites."

"We're sorry for calling you a tinker. Let us shake hands and be friends."

"Fair enough. We don't hold any grudges, we beat you fair and square."

"You are a lot tougher than that brother of yours."

"I won't let anyone hit him either."

"My name is David Byrne and this is James Kelly."

"Dixie told us your names."

They walked out of the field and down towards the village as friends.

That Monday, Michael was late getting up and his brother was already gone to serve Mass. He rushed out the door and met up with David and James, they were late as well.

"We are in for the cane this morning if we go in late."

"We will skip school for the day."

"I can't hang around here all day. My old man is the Doctor and he'd see me mitching."

"Well then, let's sneak into the school shed and take a bicycle each."

"And what will we do then?"

"Go around the country for a spin."

"All right then."

They got the bicycles and took off out the country roads and lost track of time. It was getting dark. When they were sneaking the bikes back into the shed, a hand came out of the darkness and suddenly grabbed Michael. His two friends dropped the bikes and ran. It was Brother Burke. He took Michael into the school and started beating him with a belt. Michael would not tell Brother. Burke who the other lads were, no matter how hard he hit him. He then dragged Michael all the way home where his father awaited him.

Brother Burke explained to his Father what had happened. Michael's Father began to lace the kicks and the punches into young Michael. He still wouldn't reveal the identity of the other two. This irritated his Father and made him angrier. He then got a stick and began beating him. His Mother tried to save him. At this stage the poor child could not endure much more and was in pain on the ground. To no avail, she could not save him. It was then that Patrick told his Father he had seen the boys pass the church after Mass. Michael shouted at him.

"You're a Judas, you informer."

Once again he started hitting him. It was more than Mary could take. As she sobbed, she shouted,

"Seamus, if you hit him one more time I'm leaving you and I won't come back."

An argument then broke out between the two Parents.

Seamus exclaimed, "He nearly killed you when he was born. He will be the death of you yet."

He then stormed out the door and Brother Burke followed not long after. Michael was still calling Patrick an informer, but failed to see that he was only thinking of him.

"He would have killed you. That's why I had to tell."

Mary walked him to his room where she helped him undress. She began to cry again. His body was black and blue and he was still shaking as she held him in her arms.

"Oh, my little wild boy. Why don't you be like your Brother?"

It was not long before he replied.

"I can't, Ma. Sure, he's a Saint."

He never failed to win over his Mother with the cheeky little boyish grin he always wore.

"I love you, Ma, but I hate Dad."

She told him to settle himself down.

"I will be back with some supper for you." Before leaving the room, she kissed him.

"I'll have a few words with your Father when he comes home."

He didn't come home until late. By then, the kids were asleep.

She was lying on the sofa where she intended to sleep for the night. He came into her but she wouldn't talk to him. She got up early and cooked the breakfast as normal. He got up and continued to argue.

"He's only a boy. All kids his age gets up to mischief. It's all part of growing up."

"If that's so, how come Patrick never gets into trouble? It's that traveller he is with."

"Don't you go blaming that child. He wasn't even with him. He's a nice lad. Patrick and him are like chalk and cheese. Give him time and he'll grow out of it."

The conversation ended and Seamus went off to work. The boys got up and went to school. Michael refused to walk alongside his Brother. The day ended with Patrick coming home. He was all bruised and bloodied.

"What on earth happened you?" asked his Mother.

"I told the boys at school that it was me who told Brother Burke. They were going to kill Michael so I had to stand up for him."

When his Father came home, he wanted to get the guards when he seen the state of him. Michael shouted,

"That's what happens to informers."

"It's all your fault, you little bowsie," said Seamus.

"Dad, please don't get the Guards. It is all over now."

"If they do that to you again, I will."

The following Saturday, Michael was walking into the village to meet Miley. As he passed the Midwife's cottage, Dixie was in front of him.

"Hold on there and I'll walk with you," said Michael.

"Oh, it is a good job you came," said Dixie.

"Why, what's up?"

"She stopped me and asked me to do a bit of shopping for her."

"Who stopped you?" inquired Michael.

"The Midwife and she gave me three pence for myself."

"What do you have to get her?"

"She wants one and sixpence worth of mince. And then she said that she wanted two packets of crisps. Then she shouted after me again to get her salt and vinegar. Have I enough money here to buy them?"

"How much did she give you?"

"A half a crown."

"You will have plenty in that."

"Will you come in with me and I will split the three pence with you?"

"You need not do that. Sure, I have plenty of money that I saved from the fruit picking."

"We will have to go to Jimmy's shop for those things."

"Did you see inside the cottage?"

"No, she made me wait at the door. She said her feet were killing her and she couldn't walk."

When they went into the shop, they got six packets of mints and two packets of crisps.

"How much is a packet of salt and a bottle of vinegar?" asked Dixie.

"Nine pence, to you boys."

"She gave you the exact amount of money, Dixie."

"God, she must know her prices. Thanks for coming with me I will see you later on."

"Good luck then." said Michael.

"When you're there, see if she has a bird in the cottage."

"If she lets me in."

Miley came along.

"Is that Dixie I see going up there?" asked Miley.

"Yes but it wont be long till he's back."

"Why's that?"

"When he delivers the shopping to the midwife,

just hold on a few minutes," said Michael sneer-ingly.

They watched him come running like hell and holding his head.

"What's the matter with you now? What's wrong with your head?" asked Miley.

"The mad bitch, when she seen what was in the bag she hit me with her blackthorn. It was mince meat she wanted for the dinner and two packets of salt and vinegar crisps."

Michael pissed himself laughing.

"Well, she has plenty of salt and vinegar now, the auld bag."

"You're a fucker for getting him into trouble all the time," Miley whispered to Michael.

"Ah, sure we have good fun with him. Sure, he's mad himself. He'd do anything."

"We are going up there tonight, Dixie. Meet us near the cottage at eight o'clock." said Michael.

"Right lads, I'll be waiting there. I'd love to see her talking bird."

Miley and Michael went back to the campsite and he told his Dad about Dixie.

"God, you're a little divil. I'd have loved to see her face when she opened the bag."

Maggie asked him if he had got a holy medal.

"I'll get one tonight. I forgot about it."

"Well, you make sure and get one. I don't want anything to happen to you."

That night Dixie was waiting when the lads arrived. All three of them went to her cottage. It was an old stone cottage with a hole in the side of it. The last owners removed the broken down shed that was connected to it and never replaced a stone that came off with the shed. Michael told them that he'd have a look first. She was in bed because her light was out. He sneaked up by the side where the stone was missing and looked in, she was topless. He came back and said, "Come on Dixie, the bird is in her room. I'll show you."

When they came to the hole, Michael whispered, "Look through that hole."

Miley knew what he was up to and waited for the reaction. They came running back.

"Did you see the bird?"

"Aye, a topless one with no tits."

"The cage was on her bed. Did you not see it?"

"She was scratching her tits. That's all I seen."

On the way home Michael said that they'd plan something to get her out of the house.

"It's the only way we'll find out."

"Keep an eye out for a pregnant woman."

Michael was getting worried over what Maggie

told him so he went to Patrick. He knocked on his bedroom door and walked in to his room.

"What's wrong with you?"

"Can I ask you something?"

"Yes, what do you want to know?

"Is there any such things as evil spirits?"

"Yes, I'm sure there is. Why do you ask?"

"Well, it's just that someone told me to wear a Lourdes medal so that it would keep them away."

"Any holy medal would keep away evil spirits, once you believe in it."

"But I don't have one to wear."

"I'll give you one so you won't be afraid."

"Thanks, Patrick".

He got up and went to his drawer and took out a lovely chain and medal.

"Here, let me put it around your neck."

"I'm sorry for all the things I said about you."

"That's all right. Sure, all Brothers fight. We wouldn't be a proper family if we didn't."

He threw his arms around him and said,

"I will always love you as my Brother."

"And I will always love you. Even though you are a bit wild!"

"But Mam likes you that way."

He left the room and said goodnight and thanked him for the medal. Patrick was wondering if he was all right or what had come over him. He thought that he must have been changing.

Michael decided to find out about the talking bird as the suspense was killing him. He met all the lads in the field on Saturday as a woman by the name of Lily Hogan had been expecting her first child. He did not know her but David Byrne did.

"All right then, you'll have to go to her front door and tell her she's wanted."

"I'll be waiting around her back window and when she goes out I'll get in to look."

"We will have to go around six o'clock as she goes to bed early to scratch her tits."

So the plan was put into action and they were all waiting near her cottage. Michael went around her back and the window was slightly open. He could see the budgie in the cage on her table.

"God, it must be true."

He waited and he could hear the knocking on her front door. She got up and answered it and he could hear David talking to her.

"Hold on there till I get my shawl," she said and went out the door and closed it.

He opened the window and got in and went straight for the cage. The bird bit him but he got it and put it in his pocket and out the window he went. He ran by the lads shouting to meet in the field. They all ran after him. They all sat down and then David arrived.

"I left the auld bag half way and ran."

They took out the bird and spent the next two hours trying to get the bird to talk.

"I give up," said Michael. "He must have lost his tongue."

"Ah kill him," said Miley. "Let's go home. I am freezing."

"I can't do that. Look at the size of the poor thing. It'd be cruel."

"I'll take him home and hide him," said Michael. So they all left the field and went their separate ways. When Michael got home, he put the budgie into a drawer in his press to keep it warm. Next morning coming home with his mother they met Molly crying.

"What is the matter with you, Mrs. Casey?"

"My poor Polly - she is gone! She's a divil for opening her cage to walk around. I must have left the window open. I don't know what I am going to do with out her. She was the only bit of company I had."

"It might turn up with a bit of luck."

"I don't think so. That cold weather will kill her."

"Well, anyway, we'll keep our eyes open for her. Won't we, Son?"

"Sure, Ma."

"Thank you very much but I may fear for the worst. I had her four years."

They walked on.

"The poor creature. That's all she had in the world. I feel sorry for her," said Mary. "We can count ourselves lucky having each other. That poor divil has no one."

Michael was feeling sorry now for taking the bird. "I'll have a look around for her, Ma."

"You're a very thoughtful boy son, going out of your way to help her like that."

He went to his room and the bird was still where he put it.

"Come on, I'm taking you home."

He knocked on Molly's door and when she seen her Polly in his hands she was overcome.

"Where did you find her?"

"She was in our shed. She would have been warm there."

"Come in here and I'll give you a small reward for being so kind. It's the least I can do!"

"No thanks, Mam. Looking at that smile on your beautiful face is enough for me," said Michael.

"I'll never forget this and if there is anything you ever want, come to me."

He went home feeling proud after all the trouble he caused.

CHAPTER SIX

Michael would be fourteen this Christmas and he was looking forward to it. They were all putting up the crib in front of the church with Brother Kenny. Michael was very fond of him as he was the kindest man in that school. Dixie was carrying in the animals and gently putting them down one by one.

"You like god's creatures?" Brother Kenny asked. "Have you any pets at home, Dixie?"

"Yes, I have Brother. It's a Jack Russell dog."

"How long have you got him?"

"We have him three years, Brother. He's only six months old."

The boys doubled up laughing.

"What's wrong with them, Brother?"

"Don't mind the lads, it's the way you express yourself. You always keep us happy."

On the way home Michael was telling the lads a handy way to make a few bob.

"We might be seen taking the bottles," said Miley.

"Not on a Saturday night. They're far too busy."

So they decided to swipe the empty bottles from Pat Carpenter's yard. They waited until Saturday night. It was pretty dark and they had to be quiet.

"Now remember, lads," said Michael, "You get two pence for the small ones and four pence for the large."

"David, you take James and we'll wait here until you come out. Try to get the large ones. If we see anyone we'll whistle so hide in there until they're gone away."

"But how will we know?"

"I will let a second whistle for the all clear."

So they went in and they came out carrying the bottles.

"These are heavy."

"Wait here until Dixie and myself go in. Whistle if you see any one coming."

They went in and grabbed as many bottles as they could carry and came back out.

"Let's go to the field."

"You're right. These bottles are heavy so don't drop any."

When they got to the field they discovered they had more full ones than empties.

"What are we going to do now?"

"These are all full. There is only four empty."

"We'll hide them here and come back and drink the full ones some night."

"When are we going to drink them?"

"On my birthday. It's near Christmas," said Michael. "I will meet you here tomorrow after dinner and tell you what night to drink them."

So they met in Murphy's field and discussed what night they would drink the beer.

"Christmas Eve would be the best time. They are all drunk then. No-one would notice," said Michael.

"Right then," agreed the rest.

"We will have to start early and go home around ten o'clock."

So when Christmas Eve arrived they met up again in the field. Michael did not have as much as he remembered that last time he had a drink with Miley. The other lads got stoned drunk.

"Happy birthday to you, Michael. You are a good friend," said James.

"We better be going, lads. It's getting late and they will be wondering where we are."

"Ah, fuck them," said David. "We will go when I finish this last bottle."

He drank it and they left.

"See you after Christmas, lads. Good night now and a happy Christmas to you all."

"The same to you, Michael, my friend. May you have many more good ones."

Michael arrived home with out any bother and went to bed.

"Good night, Ma. Goodnight, Pa."

The other three only got to the crib outside the church.

"I'm going to lie down here," said Dixie.

"All right," said James. "But only for a few moment's as we will have to get home."

Dixie took baby Jesus out and lay down in his place and David fell asleep over the donkey. Young James fell asleep between the two sheep and the wise men. It was Molly Casey who came on the scene as she was going to midnight Mass.

"Oh, holy Mother of God, would you look at this." Molly called to the people behind her. When they gathered she said it was a holy disgrace and she told one of the people to go and get the Priest. Father Tony came out and when he looked into the crib he nearly fainted.

"In my short time here I have never seen the likes of this."

"Will I get the guards, Father?" Molly replied.

"No, I'll send someone to get their Parents."

"I'll go," said Tom Hickey. "I know them."

"Would you look at that lad lying there and poor Jesus on the ground?"

"Go into the church out of the cold, Molly. Mass will be a bit late tonight," said Fr Tony.

"They'll burn in hell, Father. What did they think they were at?"

It was around the whole village on Christmas Day and a lot of people had a good laugh.

"Well, I'm glad you weren't with them Michael. You had the good sense to be in bed," said Seamus.

"I told you that he was a good lad, Seamus. Not like the three wise men," said Mary. "They weren't that wise to be found in a crib on Christmas Eve and the Doctor's son. I wouldn't mind that simple chap but young Byrne and Kelly should have more sense."

Well, the whole village talked about it all over Christmas and the New Year. They were known as the three wise men after their episode. They met in the field the day before they went back to school for a chat.

"What made you go in to the crib?" asked Michael. "You should have gone straight home."

"Sure, it was Dixie's fault. He wanted to go in for a lie down," said James.

"It was not my fault. We were all drunk and me Ma beat the shit out of me. I can't stay long as I have to go to the shop for some cotton balls," said Dixie.

"What the fuck do you want cotton balls for Dixie?" asked Michael. "To shove up your ass?!"

They all started to laugh.

"They're for my Mother and now my Sister wants some as well."

"Are you going to open up a teddy bear factory in your cottage or what?" asked David.

"Are you mad or what? Sure my Mother couldn't boil an egg, let alone make teddy bears. I have to get them every month for her and my sister. They won't go themselves."

"What do they do with them make snowballs?" asked James.

"I don't know. I just buy them!"

"Dixie, did you ever see your Sister naked? They're different than us they say." asked Michael.

"There's not much difference. We have a pump and they have an eye."

"How do you know that? We have no Sisters so we wouldn't know anything about it." asked Michael.

"Sure, I have seen my sister having her bath in front of the fire, in the winter nights."

"And you are telling us that she has got three eyes and we have only two." asked Miley.

"No, you fools. She has a spare eye between her legs, that's what they call it."

"But how do you know it is an eye?" asked Miley.

"Sure it winked at me a few times. I got out of bed one night to get a drink of water and walked in on my Mother."

"What was she doing?" asked Michael.

"Having a bath in front of the fire and she roared me out."

"And did you get a look at her eye?" asked David.

"Yes and it would frighten you. Hers had eyebrows!"

"I wonder where babies come from?" asked James.

"That's a mystery to me," said Michael.

"Sure, the Doctor brings it when he goes to see your mother," said Dixie.

"Sure, that's fucking stupid, what would he need the Midwife for?"

"To frighten it you out of your Mother's tummy," David replied.

"If I seen a face like that in front of me, I would never be born," said Dixie.

"Why is that?" asked James.

"She would frighten me back in. At least I would be safer in there."

"Dixie, would you know how we got into their tummies?"

"Well, my cousin told me that it was a big red headed baldy man with one eye and the only baldy man I know is the Doctor."

"Me Dad has two fucking eyes."

"I know it is not him."

"And then he tried to tell me that I went to a dance with my Father and came back home with my Mother and I were never at a dance in my life. I think my Cousin will land up in the funny farm with my Dad."

"Maybe it has something to do with her eyebrows between her legs," said James.

"It can't be," Dixie replied.

"Why not?" asked James.

"Sure they only have that to see where they're pissing."

The boys roared laughing.

"God, Dixie", said Michael. "You're some tulip. Imagine eyebrows between her legs."

"Well, I better get going as she is in a fierce temper these days. It must be the weather."

"See you, Dixie."

The boys then began singing 'Mammy, they're making eyes at me'.

It was the end of March when Father Tony gave a sermon about Easter. He reminded the people about the Easter dues as it was just around the corner.

"The good Doctor's Wife will be going around to do the collection on Easter Saturday. I would like you all to make a good effort to pay a little more this year. We're hoping to paint the church during the summer months and every little helps. Do your best and may the good Lord's blessings be on you."

When Easter Saturday came the Doctor's Wife had taken ill and she sent her Son to collect. He met up with Michael and asked him if he would go around with him.

"I have to go and see Miley but I will go to a few houses with you. You could make a right few bob for yourself," said Michael.

"How is that?" asked David.

"Well, all you have to do is take a bit of the collection yourself."

"They would find out. I was beaten black and blue over the crib."

"How would they find out? Sure no one knows what money you received."

"Well, I better be off. Here's Dixie. He'll help you out."

"I will see you later."

So David told Dixie the plan.

"Sure, I will share it out with you."

When Michael went up to see Miley he told him about the plan with David.

"But they will be caught. Sure, they read it out off the pulpit at Mass on Easter Sunday," said Miley.

"Are you sure about that?"

"I'm not certain but I'll ask Dad."

When they were having a cup of tea he asked his Father about the collection.

"God, they do, Son. That's to make a holy show out of the poor people."

"Oh shit," said Michael. "It's too late to do anything about it now."

"God, you are always putting him in the shit. He'll cop on some day," said Miley.

At Mass that Sunday Father Tony got up on the pulpit to read out the collection.

"Molly Casey, one and sixpence."

She stood up. "Hold on there you with the dog collar. I gave you a half a crown. Are you trying to show me up? One and sixpence, my arse."

"I will have to look into it. There must be some mistake."

"Yes, a big one," she replied.

When he called out the second name, the next gentleman also stood up. "I gave more than that Father."

Molly stood up again. "Who did you put in charge of this collection?"

"Mrs. Byrne, the Doctors Wife. She's a pillar to this church."

"I had a feeling he was behind all this, the big fat heap of shite."

"Molly! Your language, please! You're in the house of God."

She caused chaos until someone told Father Tony who collected the money.

"Are you telling me that the three wise men that were found in the crib are at it again?" asked Molly.

"No," replied Fr Tony. "We're now sure that there were only two boys involved, not three."

"They should be horse whipped. If I had my black thorn stick, I'd give it to them."

The poor old Doctor and his Wife were not seen in public for over two weeks. He had a long talk with the Priest and that Sunday he stood facing the crowd. He apologized and assured them that he would pay back all the money his son fiddled. David told James that some day he was going to get the better of Michael Flynn.

"Look at all the trouble he got me into. He knew that they would read it out in church."

"But how would he know?" asked James. "You want to be careful not to blame him if he didn't know."

"His older brother is the top altar boy and is well

in with Father Tony. He knew all right." There was hate brewing in David's mind but he would bide his time and still be friends.

It was the start of May and it was time for the missions it would last the full week. The Brothers would line up all the boys and they would march to the church. Michael loved to hear them talk about the strange places they had travelled to. They told stories about the living conditions of those strange people. But most of all, he knew that all the men would go in the evening after work.

They would go to the public bar after the missions and he could stay out late. The nights he would not go out he would read his comics by the open fire. He loved the 'Dan Dare' comics as they were all about going to the moon. He would read books all about the American west, 'The Cowboy's and Indians'.

Most of all he loved the 'Our Boys' that were sold in the Christian Brother's school. They would come out every month but he also got the Dandy and the Topper every week. He loved reading those books and would then pass them on to Miley to read. It was Friday, the last day of the missions, when the Missionary stood up on the pulpit.

"Now, boys, as this is the last day of the missions, we'll talk about the black babies. We'll be setting up collection boxes in the schools to collect money for them. All we ask is that if you have any spare pennies, you would put them in the boxes. When they are full, the Brothers will send out the money to us to help those children."

Dixie stood up in the church and Brother Burke kept telling him to sit down. He would not sit down and the missionary asked him what was the matter with him.

"Well, Father, how could there be black babies?"

"Well, Son, it's the color of their skin."

"Well," said Dixie. "When my skin is black, I use soap and water to wash it off. Have they no soap?"

At this point all the boys were laughing and even Brother Burke could not help a smile. He was still trying to get him to sit when Father Tony explained to the missionary about him.

"Son, in time to come you will understand about the black babies. But in the meantime if you have any spare pennies, put them in the box. You're good father in heaven will reward you for putting your pennies in the box."

On the way back to the school, Dixie said that the missionary was a fool.

"But why is that?" one of the boys asked.

"There's no such thing as black babies. And I am

not putting my pennies in any box. I told him all he needs is a bar of soap."

No one could get it into his head about the black babies. He wouldn't believe it. When the boys sat down to their dinner that night they busted out laughing.

"What is so funny?" their father asked. "The two of you seem to be in great form."

So they told him about Dixie and what he said to the missionary. Their Father was drinking some tea and it went up his nose from the laughter. Their Mother was in stitches.

"God, poor old Dixie. What a character!" she said.

It was the start of the summer holidays and everyone was glad that school had finished. Michael and Miley went fruit picking again and David and James Kelly joined them. He had to pay back his Father the money he fiddled from the parish collection. The dancing boards were in full swing at the crossroads and Mary had promised Michael that she would take him.

There was a carnival set up this year. When they arrived the place was packed out, with children all over the place. She went and sat in the same spot where she first met her Husband and Joe.

"It was right here, Son, that I met your father and Joe."

"You should have left him here," said Michael.

"Sure, then you would not be around."

"Why did you not take to Joe? He's very nice."

"But your Father was the most handsome man here. Even though he couldn't dance."

"He was too mean to dance, in case he wore out the leather on his shoes," said Michael sniggering. "Is this where Sally met Joe?"

"Yes. Sure, Sally and myself were childhood friends. We went everywhere together and we started courting from here every Saturday. God, the music is beautiful, Son. Come and have a dance with me."

"But Ma, I can't dance."

"Are you afraid to wear out the leather in your shoes?" laughed his Mother.

"Come on then, just one dance but you will have to teach me."

"I taught your Dad."

It was a slow waltz and she put her arms around him, and it brought memories.

"God, you're a handsome boy, just like your Father. Do you come here often?" asked his Mum laughing.

When they finished they went and got into the bumpers at the carnival. They had such good fun. They heard a shout and Miley was waving to them.

"Come on, Ma. Let's go to the stalls and try and win something. There are some nice things there."

Miley joined them.

"Did your Parents not come?" asked Mary.

"Oh, they're here somewhere."

They met the Doctor and his Wife and David as well.

"How are you Mary?"

"Oh, grand and yourself?"

"We are not too bad either. It's a beautiful day for the carnival."

"Were you in the bumpers yet, David?"

"No, Mam. I have to stay with my Parents."

"Well, you know the trouble he got into. We have to watch him now."

"It is all part of growing up. Sure, they didn't commit murder or anything."

Next thing they heard a voice behind them, it was the bold Molly Casey. She saw the Doctor and came straight over.

"God, is this your Wife, baldy?"

"Yes, Molly. This is Joan."

"What the hell did you see in him? He's useless!"

"It must have taken you a few hours to get here,

carrying that weight. And who might this tall boy be?"

"This is my Son, David."

"God, no wonder you are over twenty stone. This poor lad is like a lamppost. I saw more meat on a tinkers stick after a good fight. No wonder he fiddled the collection. Well, I best be off. Poor Polly will be wondering where I got to."

She looked at Michael. "God, it's you. A grand lad. It was this boy who found my Polly and brought her back. The kindest poor creature in the village. I brought him into this world and I'm glad I did. Well, good luck now!" she said and away she went about her business.

"I will see you again, Doctor. I hope you enjoy the carnival."

"You too, Mary."

"You never told me that you found Molly's Budgie. Where did you find it?"

"It's a long story, Ma, but someday I'll tell you all about it."

When they went to the stalls they met Dan and Maggie and Lassie was there too. He jumped up on her when he saw her.

"How are you two getting on? Any luck yet?"

"No, Mrs. Flynn. Sure, we only tried once. It's hard to win at these places. It's a racket."

Michael bought a few tickets and the next thing his number came up.

"Good on you, son. Pick out something nice for yourself."

He had a look around and seen a beautiful picture. It was of the Virgin Mary.

"Can I take that, please?"

The man handed it to him.

"Oh that is beautiful. What do you think Dan?"

"It is the nicest picture I seen yet."

"You may get Father Tony to bless it for you, as it will always bring you luck."

"But I am giving it to my Mother. It will be the first beautiful thing I give her."

"Oh Son, I will treasure this for the rest of my life and I will have it blessed next week."

Miley let a shout that his number came up too and asked his mother to pick out something nice.

"Are you two lads on the fiddle or what? We can't win a thing. It must be beginners luck."

They walked back into the village together with Lassie at their heels.

"Mam, how did she know we were gone to the carnival?"

"A dog watches everything, Son."

"Well, goodbye now. We will see you again sometime."

"See you, Mrs. Flynn."

"I will call up tomorrow, Miley, after my dinner. Good luck, Dan. Bye, Maggie."

Michael arrived up at Dan's on Sunday and they took Lassie for a walk.

"I'm not going to spend all summer picking fruit, Miley."

"No, sure, we want a break before we go back to school."

"Yes, we can go swimming and do a bit of fishing. Let's go for a swim now."

So they walked up to the stream.

"Look at all those trout. It's a pity we have no net."

"We must make one sometime and clean out this stream."

"That's a good idea."

"That David looks like a girl. Would you think so, Miley?"

"I know one thing and that's never to trust him. I'd say he is a right hangman."

"Well, he never hung me over the crib or over the collection."

"Well, watch your back with him. I wouldn't trust him as far as I could throw him."

"I haven't seen poor Dixie. I wonder where he went to?"

"Well, I don't think David gave him too much money out of the fiddle."

"He has to work now to pay the money back to his Father, the gobshite."

"Sure, he's a Mother's boy. They won't take his money off him."

"Come on, let's swim before it gets too cold."

And when they were naked, Lassie jumped in too. They dried off on the bank and headed back home.

"Good luck, Miley. I will see you in the morning in the village."

CHAPTER SEVEN

They worked up to the end of July as they had enough money made. For the next three weeks, they had a great time swimming and fishing. David Byrne and James Kelly met Michael in the village.

"Are you not working now?"

"No, we are having this week to ourselves."

"We will be going back to school next week so we are going fishing every day. Why don't you come with us one day before we start back to school?"

"I go fishing with Miley as we always go together."

"Sure, bring him with you."

"Right then, I'll ask him when I go up to the campsite."

"Ok, meet us here on Friday, as we are going up to the fast water. Plenty of trout there."

When he saw Miley he told him. "I have to go with

Mam and Dad that day. If you are going up to the fast water, watch yourself. It is deadly dangerous."

"I might not go with them. I prefer to go fishing with you and we do well enough."

Michael did not go to meet the lads that Friday, instead he took Lassie up to Sally's. He loved holding the little baby and making her laugh.

"Emma is beautiful Sally."

"Yes, she will be the only child I will ever have and I adore her. You will be going back to school next week."

"I know. I hate the thoughts of it."

"It won't be that long till you are off for Halloween and then there's Christmas."

"That's my favorite time of the year as I have my birthday as well."

"I hope you don't land up in the crib like your friends did last year!"

"There will be no fear of that Sally. Sure, I have more sense than that lot."

"How is your friend Miley keeping?"

"He's grand, the best friend I have."

"Well, your Mother is very fond of him. He's a lovely chap to talk to. God, there's a family that have nothing and yet they are never in trouble."

"They're a very happy family. Sure, you never hear

Dan giving out to Maggie. Well I best be off, Sally. I only took Lassie for a walk. Good bye then."

"Goodbye, Michael and don't forget to call again."

"I won't."

Michael went back home and listened to the radio for the night.

When they went back to school they met back up with Dixie.

"Where were you? We haven't seen you since the start of the holidays," asked Michael.

"Sure the auld one brought us down the country to stay with our cousins for the holidays."

"And did you have a good time?"

"Ah, it was alright but I was glad to get back home. They're all mad down there. My cousin learned me how to make a catapult and we spent all of our time killing birds."

"Ah, you didn't kill the poor little birds, Dixie?"

"No, I wouldn't do that. I only killed the dirty crows."

"Then, you must show us how to make them then and we can go after the crows too," suggested Miley.

"I'll meet you in Murphy's field around four o'clock and I'll show you then."

The boys already knew how to make a catapult but they just wanted to have the craic with Dixie.

They met in the field that evening and Dixie showed them his catapult. Michael asked him where he got the elastic.

"I got it out of a girl's knickers."

"How did you manage that?"

"I took one of the girl's I met down there into the woods and I laid her down on some dry leaves."

"Yeah and what did you do next?" asked Michael.

"I lifted up her dress and took off her knickers."

"You did not!" said Miley, in disbelief.

"I did and then I took the elastic out of it and ran away."

"Why did you run away though?"

"I didn't want to kiss her. I only wanted to get into her knickers, you eejits."

"Who was she?" asked Miley.

"Her name was Lizzie and I was very fond of her."

"Did you ever have a wet dream about her?" asked Michael.

"I did and when I woke up the next morning, it was raining."

"But that's not a wet dream," laughed Michael.

"It was because I dreamed about her standing in the rain."

The boys were enjoying this.

"Ok so, well did you ever take her for a walk?"

"Yes, we went down to the Farmer's field one day and she pointed out to this animal."

"Yeah Dixie, keep going," smirked Michael.

"She told me it was a bull. I asked her how she knew it was a bull and she told me it was because he had a pump between his legs like me. I said there was no way it was a pump, that it was more like a cannon. It was huge. And then she asked me if I would be her bull."

"And what did you say?" asked Miley sniggering.

"I told her that I couldn't be a bull because I had no horns."

"Yeah, Dixie, you're right," agreed Miley.

"You know Dixie, you'd be better off breaking windows with that catapult and leave the poor crows alone," suggested Michael.

"I think you're right there, Michael. The first would have to be Paraffin Joe. He slapped me in the face, the auld fucker."

"Yeah and you could do the school as well and we'd get a few days off because they'd have to repair them," sniggered Michael.

"Jaysus, you's are right. I'm going to start tonight."

"Right so," said Miley. "Sure, we'll see you tomorrow in school."

When Michael and Miley arrived in school next

morning and were told to go home. Every window in the school was smashed. Not only the school but also Paraffin Joe's house got it as well. Worse still, Dixie got him with a stone on the head and he was sent to hospital.

"Holy God, Michael, I didn't think that he would believe us."

"Look at Guard Swan over there? If he knows it was Dixie, he's done for."

On the way home they met up with Dixie and he was breaking his heart laughing. The boys weren't, as they knew this was serious. However, they were a bit pleased to get the rest of the week off school. They told Dixie to meet them in the woods so they wouldn't be seen. In the woods, Michael informed Dixie that Guard Swan and Guard O'Neill would be out looking for the lad who had done it.

"Ah well, they'll have to catch me first because I'm going to dig a hole in Murphy's field."

"Why are you going to do that?"

"To set a trap and if they follow me, they'll fall into it."

"Well," said Michael. "If you keep quiet they won't find out. Don't go blabbing to anyone about it."

"Ok boys, I've just got one more window to break first."

"Whose window, Dixie?"

"Jimmy Griffin's. He's a miserable auld fucker."

"Don't do that," advised Michael. "It's right beside the Garda station."

"Ah, don't worry, meet me in Murphy's field tomorrow morning and I'll let you's know how I got on."

They separated. Next morning all the boys gathered in Murphy's field and Dixie had a huge hole dug.

"Oh Holy Mother, Dixie, how long have you been digging this?"

The two of them jumped into it.

"It's deep, Dixie. It's up to my chest," said Michael. "What are you going to do now?"

"See all that pig shit and cow dung over there, I'm filling it with that. Now that you's are here, you's can help me."

They helped him and when the hole was almost full they threw a few buckets of water into it. They then gathered plenty of rotten sticks and put them across the hole. Then they covered it with grass and leaves as a disguise.

"Now if they follow me they're in for a surprise."

They looked back as they were walking away and their swamp blended in perfectly with the field.

"I'm hitting Jimmy Griffins at dinner hour tomorrow. See you's later, lads."

"Yeah Dixie, see you tomorrow."

"God Michael, he's cracking up. What did they do to him on holidays?"

Dixie didn't wait until tomorrow. When the boys arrived back into the village, they heard an awful commotion. Dixie then ran passed them, followed by Guard Swan and Guard O'Neill. Then came a load of lads and lassies, mad to see what was happening. Michael saw James and he asked him what happened.

"He broke all of the windows out of Griffins shop and when he finished, he broke a window out of the Garda station as well."

"Look at him go, Miley. Come on, he's heading for the field."

The boys began to run after them. Dixie cleared the gate to the field and then slowed down a bit. When the Guards were catching up, he took up speed and flew off again. Dixie cleared the swamp but the Guards behind fell into it. Dixie cleared the next gate and vanished. Everyone was in the field now, bursting with laughter.

"Holy man, look at them! They're up to their waist in pig shit!"

The kids couldn't contain their laughter as the two Guards walked slowly back to the village covered in shit. Even Jimmy Griffin was laughing, after they passed his broken window.

The following Monday, the boys went back to school curious about what happened with Dixie. They were then informed that Dixie had gone.

"But where is he gone to Brother Kenny?"

"He is in the mental hospital. We will miss him. He was not a bad lad but his auld mind wasn't working properly."

"But why did they put him into the mental?"

"For lots of reasons. After he broke the windows, the guards went round to his house and he left Guard Swan in a heap on the floor. He even attacked his poor Mother. Hopefully they'll be able to cure him and he can come back home to us soon."

"God, I am sorry now for ripping him off at the fruit picking. I feel bad about it," said Michael.

"I was wondering why we never saw him. Imagine putting him in the mental. Remember the mincemeat and the oil and when he told Brother Kenny about his dog? God we pissed ourselves laughing. We will have no one now to have fun with."

The weather was getting very rough now with plenty of rain and high winds. Michael would stay in and read his books and spend time with his Brother. Mary was delighted to see them getting on together; it was not always that way. He seen a big change in him in the last year, even his Dad noticed it. He seemed to be more grown up and that was a good sign. Miley told him at school that he would be going away again for the weekend.

"Where do you go to?"

"Down to see a very old woman, my Dad's Aunt. I met a girl down there. We are only friends at the moment but she is beautiful."

"That's great. I'm very happy for you. When am I going to meet her?"

"Don't worry. When it's time. I'd like you to be my best man"

"No problem, I'd be delighted. Is it true the best man has the first night?"

"You must be joking. You want jam on both sides. You're my best friend since we started school and without you I would have been lost."

"I will be your friend for life, Miley. I just hope you settle down in this village. Your Dad and Mam would be lost if you had to move somewhere else to live."

"I was born here and my Grand parents are buried here, so this is my home."

It was October when Miley went away for the weekend and Michael got bored at home. He took Lassie into the village and met up with David and James.

"Why don't you come fishing with us tomorrow? We are going after Pike."

"Right then, I have nothing else to do. It will pass a few hours."

"Where is your friend Miley? Sure, he could come as well, the more the merrier."

"He's gone away for the weekend. He'll be back on Sunday night for school".

"Well, meet us here at one as I have to buy some fishing line."

Michael went home and prepared his fishing rod, he put stronger line on the spool. He met the boys and they headed for the Barrow track. They were soon up near the weir.

"Look at that current with all the rain. It's nearly flooded. We will have to use more lead."

They were there about two hours and never even got a bite and were getting bored.

"I am going to sit down here for a while and then I am going home. It is useless," said Michael.

He sat down and put his legs over the bank and the other two started messing about. There was a splash and he saw James in the water.

"Help me, I can't swim!"

Michael got up to take off his clothes but the strong current was sweeping him away.

"Hurry up, he's drowning. Oh please, don't let him drown!"

"You run and get some help straight away," said Michael. "I will try and catch him further down. Don't stand there, run like hell and get some help."

David took off. Michael ran down the bank but James had disappeared, there was no sign of him. It was at least twenty minutes before David arrived with two men.

"It's too late, he's gone. There was nothing I could do to save him. The water was too fast."

Michael sat down crying as one of the men went for the Guards. They radioed for help before they left the station and a few divers arrived later on. The boys were taken to the village station and questioned separately about the incident. Their Parents were told to come to the station right away. Father Tony was called and told about the tragedy and asked to inform James' Parents.

"I will have to send one of my men with you, Jimmy. You go with the Priest."

The search went on until it got to dark.

"We will have to resume the search in the morning."

David told the guards that Michael had a row with James and threw him into the water while Michael gave a true description of what really happened.

The Guards did not believe Michael and told him that he was lying.

"I am not lying. What I told you is the honest truth. David is lying about this."

"But why would he lie? After all he is the Doctor's Son and we don't believe you."

They let David go and as he was going out the door he said to Michael,

"You drowned James."

"I did not, David. Why are you saying this about me? You know the truth, so tell them."

He walked out the door with his Parents and never looked back.

"Michael, Son, are you telling them the truth?"

"Yes, Ma. I am not lying, honestly."

"I knew it would come to this. You are always getting into trouble. I warned you."

Seamus stuck into him then.

"Why won't you believe your own Son? He is no killer," said Mary.

"How can I after all the things he done?"

"Even my own Father will not believe me." Michael started to cry.

"If you did not go around with them tinkers, this wouldn't happen."

"They had nothing to do with this. They're my best friends. You shouldn't say that."

Mary asked the Guard what would happen now. Would they send him away?

"Well, the courts will decide that, but it's looking pretty bad."

They let Michael home with his Parents; he was still insisting that he did not do it. They recovered James body the next afternoon and the whole village was in shock. Miley returned home and was shocked to hear about the tragedy. How could this happen? Dan and Maggie were stunned when their son told them the sad news.

"Poor Michael, what is he going to do now?"

"I told you, Dan. I seen evil around him," said Maggie.

"I don't believe that Michael is capable of doing such a thing and I will stand by him. David Byrne has got something to do with this and I will find out sooner or later."

The school would remain closed until young James Kelly was laid to rest. His wake was held in his own home and they carried his coffin to the church. Mary and her Son, Patrick, attended his funeral but Seamus or Michael could not face it. James' Mother and Father came over to Mary and Patrick.

"I'm not blaming your Son for this tragedy and I don't believe what they tell me. It was God's way that he should end his life like this. There's no one to blame."

Mary thanked her and they hugged each other in the graveyard.

It was Tuesday when the school re-opened and Michael attended, he wasn't afraid. They all knelt down and said a prayer for the soul of James Kelly. Michael told Miley exactly what had happened.

"I told you not to trust him."

None of the other boys would talk to him as David had poisoned their minds with lies. After school they all jumped him, Miley tried to help him but there were too many. They beat Michael until he was unconscious and only that the Midwife appeared, he was dead. They all ran but she got a few of them with her stick.

"We'll get him again," they shouted.

She told Miley to go and get the Doctor and be quick about it. The Doctor arrived and the Midwife had her shawl beneath his head.

"We have got to get this child home as quick as possible. He's in danger."

Dan arrived on the scene and his son told him what happened. He was mad. He picked up Michael in his arm as Miley ran ahead to notify his Mother. She ran out and saw Dan and the Doctor approaching with her Son.

"Oh God, what did they do to my baby. How bad is he?"

"We won't know until I have a good look at him but he's pretty bad."

They took him to his room and his mother wept when she seen the state of him. When the Doctor examined him he came back out and told her that he was critical.

"We will not know anything for the next few days. Pray to God he pulls through."

Dan and Miley had to leave. They didn't want any trouble from his Father.

"Thank you, Dan, for bringing him home. He looks on you as his second family."

"We will pray for him tonight. It will kill Maggie when she hears this. She loves him like her own. I will call back during the week when his father is not around. I don't want to cause any trouble."

The Doctor sat down and told Mary that if his Son was involved in this that he would kill him.

"I know you and your family a long time, Mary, and I will not fall out with you over this. We don't know what happened up at that river. My Son could be lying."

"We won't fall out, Doctor. No matter what happens we will always be friends."

"If he gets any worse, send for me straight away."

"I will, Doctor, and thank you."

Young Patrick heard about what happened when he left the church and ran home.

"How is he, Ma?" He was crying.

"I don't know if he will pull through or not. Get your bike and go to the mill and tell your Father to come home straight away."

He went out the door and was back with his Father and Joe in no time. They went into his room and Mary was crying calling Michael to wake up.

"God, what a shower of scumbags done this to him? If I find out, I'll kill them."

"Now, will you back up your son instead of listening to every ones gossip?"

"She's right, Seamus. No-one knows the truth yet and what is not right will come to light."

"I am going down to report this to the Guards. I hope they will find the culprits."

Joe went with him as Patrick and his Mother prayed at his bedside. She stayed up all night with him, with her Husband at her side. He did not go to work the next day; they just waited and hoped that he would wake up. Father Tony came to the cottage and prayed with them, he could not believe what he seen. Michael woke up after the third day.

"Hi, Ma!"

"Oh, my baby, are you all right?"

"I feel all right. What day is it?"

"It's Friday, Son. You have been asleep since Tuesday."

"I am starving!"

"Hold on there till I call your Dad!"

Seamus came to his room and cried. "Who done this terrible deed to you Son? So I can get them arrested."

"I will not inform on anyone Dad. I'd rather die first, so leave it at that."

"I can't make you out, Son, to allow those hooligans to get away with this."

"I done nothing wrong. If I could have saved James I would. The water was too fast."

"I know that now, Son. Forgive me for being too rough on you and for been stupid."

"You're not stupid, Dad and there is nothing to forgive, but don't blame Dan for this. Mam told me that it was him that carried me home. I'd love to thank him."

"And you will, Son. I promise you that."

"Thanks, Dad. I hope they don't send me away."

"You just get better. I want to see you running around the place."

"Where is Lassie?"

"I will go and get her for you now; your Mother is cooking some food for you." "Thanks, Dad. I really do love you and I adore both of you and I am sorry about the past."

Mary came in with the food to him while his Father went out to get Lassie.

"Ma, Dad and I made it up. What changed him?" he asked.

"Whatever Joe said to him when they talked."

Michael was over the moon when Lassie came into his room and jumped up on his bed.

"That dog loves you Son. Let him stay in with you until you feel a bit better."

Mr. and Mrs. Kelly called to the cottage to find out if he was well. Mary brought them down to his room and they sat and talked to him.

"I did not do that to your Son. David Byrne is lying and some day the truth will come out."

"We know that Son and I hope those boys that done this to you are caught."

"Thank you for calling here and I am so sorry for what happened to James."

"That is all right, Son. He is resting with God now. He's at peace."

CHAPTER EIGHT

Seamus took a walk up to the campsite and when Dan saw him coming, he stood up.

"I don't want any trouble, Sir."

"It's all right. Dan. I didn't come here to cause trouble. I came here to thank you and your family for been so kind to my Son. I was wrong about you, in fact, I was wrong about my Son as well. Forgive me."

"There is no need for that, Sir. We are very fond of Michael. To us, he's family."

Maggie got up. "Would you like a cup of tea, Sir?"

"On one condition, call me Seamus." He looked up at Miley and said, "Thank you for standing up for him."

"He stood by me when I started school and your Wife has been very kind to us."

"I would like to ask you something, if you don't mind."

"Ask away, Seamus. Whatever we can do, we will be more than happy to help you."

"Michael is asking for you and I would be honored if you call in and see him."

"We would really love to see him and I would love to get those boys that done this to him. Mr. Flynn, Michael would never do a thing like that. He's innocent."

"I know that now but the courts could take a different view. Who are they going to believe? David's Father is a Doctor and I am only a Labourer so you know what will happen."

"I understand what you are saying, but please God the truth comes out before the court."

"I hope so. It would kill his Mother if they sent him away. He is her pride and joy. Well, I better be going and thank you for your time and for the tea."

"It was a pleasure. It's a pity I couldn't offer you more. Tell Michael that we will call in to see him soon."

He got up and Dan offered to walk with him as far as the village. On the way back Seamus said, "We must have a drink sometime?"

"Maybe you will call out some night and we can have a few there," said Dan.

"I'd like that. Well, goodnight, Dan. It was a pleasure talking to you."

"Goodnight to you too and safe home."

At church the next day, Father Tony talked about what happened to Michael.

"I want to make it clear that who ever did this cruel deed are only animals. They left that child in a critical condition and it nearly cost him his life. We buried one child here through an awful tragedy and we very nearly buried another. I want this to stop now, before something evil happens. There are Mothers and Fathers here. It was some of your Sons that were involved." He continued, "Young James Kelly is at rest now and he wouldn't want this to happen again. I beg you not to harm this boy again or you will have to answer to God."

Dan and his family called in to see Michael and his Mother was delighted. When they entered his room Michael's eyes lit up, he was so happy to see them.

"I'll be back at School next week, Dan and thank you for bringing me home."

"You just get better and don't worry about School. Why don't you tell on these animals?"

"I could never do that. Then I would be worse than David Byrne."

Mary brought them in tea and biscuits and sat with them and talked.

"I am scared for him. What if it happens again? He has been hurt enough."

"I think they learned their lesson. Just in case, I will be waiting for him after School from now on," said Dan.

Michael returned to School. The weather was getting worse with rain and wind. Brother Burke called him into his office and begged him to point out the boys.

"I can't do that, Brother, no matter what happens."

"They could have killed you."

"I know the whole village is against me but I swear I am innocent."

"Well, I will attend the court next week and do everything possible for you."

"Thank you, Brother. I would appreciate that. I don't want to be sent away."

When he walked out with Miley, Dan was waiting for them to walk him home.

When his Father arrived home that night, he was cut and bruised.

"What ever happened to you, Seamus?" asked Mary.

"I just fell off my bike on the way home."

"Well, sit down here and I will clean you up."

"They are only scratches, love. I am all right."

"They look nasty enough."

She knew that this was no accident. When they went to bed later on that night, she asked him to tell her the truth.

"I didn't want to frighten Michael but they are still calling him a killer. It's bad enough with lads his own age saying it but grown ups are worse."

"Is that what caused all those cuts and bruises?"

"Yes, I hit one of them."

"God, what are we going to do? There is a lot of hate against Michael in this village."

Michael was listening to everything, he was up getting a drink. He went back to bed and cried his eyes out and asking himself, 'Why are they doing this to me?'

Dan was sick the next day and when Michael came out of School, they attacked him again. It was not as bad as the last time but Miley got the same for backing him up. Miley still walked home with his friend. When Michael's Mother seen them both, she cried. She made Miley stay in her house until her Husband came in, to bring him home.

"When is this going to stop?" asked Mary.

"It's going to get worse as the days go by."

"Come on, Son. I will take you home. Are you sure you are all right?"

"Yes, Mr. Flynn. It was Michael they hit the most. I was trying to save him."

When Maggie seen him she called Dan, she knew there was something wrong. He was never this late coming home from School.

"How is Michael? I hope they did not hurt him too much."

"He's sore enough but it wasn't as bad as the first time. I wish this would stop altogether."

When Dan came out and seen his Son, he insisted on Miley telling him who the boys were.

"I can't tell you, Dad. I'd be letting down my best friend and I can't do that!"

"But they are going to hurt the two of you every chance they get. Can you not understand? Look, what happened today happened because I was sick and couldn't be there. What is going to happen tomorrow, Son, or the next day? We will have to stop them."

"Your Father is right, Miley. They don't know when to stop."

"All right then if this happens one more time, I'll give you all their names."

"You're doing the right thing, Son. They have done enough to your friend already."

"Thanks, son," Seamus added. "I better be on my way this rain is getting heavier."

"Good night, Seamus and thank your Wife for looking after our Son."

Michael had gone to bed when his Father arrived home, he was soaking wet.

"Get out of those wet clothes before you are down with the flu. How are Dan and Maggie?"

"Dan was in bed when I called up. He was not feeling too well, stomach trouble. Maggie was waiting on Miley and knew that something had happened."

"How is he?"

"He went to bed early. He's feeling a bit sore. Will this ever stop, love?"

"If it happens again, young Miley is going to name all those involved."

"Good on him. It's about time they were stopped in their tracks."

"There's tea made in the pot. I'm going to see if he's all right."

She went to his room and sat beside him on his bed. "Don't go to school tomorrow, son."

"I have to Ma or they will think that they got the better of me. I'll be all right. I love you, Ma and I promise you that no-one will ever hurt me again. Is Patrick home yet?"

JOHN CODY

"He should be here any minute. I'll send him down to you when he arrives. I will go and get his dinner ready and I will come in later with a drink for you."

When Patrick arrived home he went straight in to see his Brother.

"Are you all right?"

"Yes, I am fine and I will be back in school tomorrow, just to show them I'm not afraid."

"Be careful. You know David Byrne is behind all this. He's telling the boys to get you."

"That's because I knocked the shit out of him in Murphy's field" said Michael. "He's also saying that they will beat the shit out of you when they get you to that school."

"That is what I am afraid of. Dan told Miley everything about that place. It's brutal."

"Well, don't let it bother you. Father Tony and Brother Burke are going to stand by you."

"I'd rather kill myself than be sent there. Miley told me too much about it."

"Well, get some rest and I'll see you tomorrow after school as I am serving early Mass. Goodnight, Michael, I have to get out of these wet clothes or I will be in bed sick tomorrow."

When Mary and Seamus went to bed, she told him that she ordered a bike for Michael's birthday.

"That's great. I will pay half of it for him. He deserves something nice."

"I am worried about that court case next week. What is going to happen him?"

"I don't know love but it is going through my mind every day since this happened."

"Will it ever end? There are so many vicious people in this village."

"I hope so but one thing is for sure, we will know who our friends are."

Michael was up before his father went out to work next morning. It was lashing rain.

"God, this weather is getting worse. Patrick will be soaked before he gets to the church," Seamus sighed.

"Is he gone already, Dad?"

"Yes, you know him, always has to be early for Mass. Well, I better go. Joe will be waiting down the lane. Goodbye, love. Take care, Son."

"I will, Dad. Tell Joe I was asking for him. I love you, Dad."

"And I love you too, Son."

"Michael, wrap up warm! This rain is down for the day."

He went to his room and came back out with his school bag and gave Lassie a hug.

"I am going, Ma!"

"Well, give me a kiss before you go."

He gave her a big hug and kiss and told her that he loved her.

"And I love you too, Son. Be careful and get someone to walk you home."

"Don't worry, Ma. I will be all right."

It was still raining that evening when Patrick arrived home. He was soaked.

"Get out of them wet clothes and give yourself a good drying off or you'll catch a cold," she shouted down to him. "Did you pass your Brother on the way home?"

"I didn't see him all day and I was surprised to see young Miley walking home alone."

She knew instantly that there was something wrong. Miley walking home alone? Never.

"Patrick, I'm going up to see Dan. All of your dinners are in the oven. Tell your Father where I am gone."

"You will get soaked in that rain, Ma."

She went out the door with Lassie at her heels. She hurried to the camp.

"Hello, Mrs. Flynn. What are you doing out in this weather? There is a storm brewing."

"Have you seen Michael? He was not at school today."

"I thought he wasn't well," said Miley.

"Oh God Almighty, they must have got him on the way to School. I will look around for him."

"Hold on there and we will go with you. He can't be that far. He could have gone home."

"I will go to the cottage first. Dan, you could be right."

When they reached the cottage her Husband was home.

"What's wrong love?"

"Miley told me he wasn't at School."

"Who?"

"Your Son, of course. They must have got him. He left here this morning and never reached the school. There's something wrong. They could have beaten him up and dumped him somewhere."

"Patrick and Miley, you take one end of the village. Dan, you come with me and I'll get Joe. Maggie, I want you to stay here with Mary, just in case he turns up."

"I will, don't worry!"

They went to Joe's cottage and told him what happened.

"I'll get my Dad as well."

They searched the village from top to bottom, but could not locate him. They arrived back to the cottage to see had he turned up but he hadn't.

Patrick and his Mother were crying as Maggie tried to console them.

"I am going to notify the Guards, love."

"And I will go with you," offered Joe. "Dad, stay here. We won't be long," Joe said to his father.

"I will make a pot of tea for them."

The Guards told him that they would have to wait twenty-four hours in case he turned up.

"I know some of those boys got him on the way to school. Why do we have to wait?"

"In case he has decided to stay with a friend. It happens all the time."

"He has no friends since that tragedy. They nearly killed him last week."

"All right then, I will send out a patrol to search for him but I want to know these boys' names."

"I don't know what their names are but I can ask his only friend. He's at the cottage."

They returned to the cottage and Seamus asked Miley if he would give their names.

"Ok, Mr. Flynn, get some paper and write them down." He gave the names. They included David Byrne.

They stayed up all night and the Guards came around and took the names of the boys. Seamus thanked Dan and Maggie for helping.

"We're not finished yet, not until we find him."

Joe cycled out to the mill to let his boss know and then came back to the cottage. They all resumed the search next morning and his boss arrived with all his men to lend a hand. It was a young Guard who discovered Michael's school bag and topcoat. They were beside the Barrow. There were signs of a scuffle and shoe marks leading into the water. He called in the rest of the force and notified the next town for divers. Mary collapsed when she heard the news.

"They have killed my baby." They sent for the Doctor. She was so bad that he had to sedate her.

CHAPTER NINE

Mary woke up to the sound of the Dog barking. She was still holding his photograph. Her husband was standing over her.

"Are you all right, love?"

"Yes, those tablets must have put me to sleep. God, I forgot to make your dinner. The Guards were here early this morning. They've found a body."

"Is it Michael?"

"They won't know for a few weeks. Oh, what am I going to do?"

"Come on into the sitting room and I will make you a nice cup of tea."

"I'll get up and make you a dinner first. You must be starving."

"Don't worry, I'll make a bit myself. Come on now into the sitting room."

"Make up Lassie some food. The poor thing must be starving. Are you all right there?"

"Yes, grand. Come here, Lassie, your food is in your dish."

Seamus came in with two cups of tea. Handing his Wife one, he asked her what the Guard had said.

"Two fishermen discovered the skeleton of a young male below the riverbank. The Guard said that it was in the water a long time and they had to send to Dublin for an examination. This medal was around the neck of the skeleton and they asked if it was Michael's."

"I never seen him wearing any medals so don't worry, it couldn't be him."

"I'll have to ask Patrick, because I know that he had a couple in his wardrobe. "When you think back to all the names poor Miley gave. They were no good. They all had an alibi."

"The poor lad is gone down to live with his aunt now and broke his parent's hearts."

"What else could he do? They would have been after him for giving the names."

"Listen, go and put on your coat and we will take Lassie for a walk."

"Where will we go?"

"Up to see Dan and Maggie. We haven't seen them for ages."

Dan knew who it was the minute Lassie ran over to him and stepped out to have a look.

"Look, Maggie, we have company. Here comes Seamus and Mary. It's grand to see you both. Come in here and sit down. Put on the auld kettle, love."

"Did you hear any news?" asked Seamus.

"No, I didn't. I wasn't around the village all week."

"They pulled out the body of a young boy early this morning from the Barrow."

"God, Maggie, I was right. I heard a lot of commotion early this morning but I didn't bother getting up. It wasn't young Michael, was it?"

"We don't know, Dan. We have to wait till we talk to Patrick. They wanted to know if he wore one of these," Seamus said, handing him the medal.

"God, I think he did. Maggie told him his fortune once and she had seen a dark cloud over him."

"Well, he told us that he was going to get one off his Brother but I never saw him wear one."

"And are you sure that you never saw a medal around his neck?"

"Never," replied Maggie. "The only lad that would tell you that would be Miley, if he was here. We miss him a lot. He's coming back shortly with his girlfriend so we can get to know her."

"Well, we will just have to wait and see what

happens next and that's the worst part," said Seamus.

"I hate this waiting and wondering if it is him or not. I will be a nervous wreck," said Mary.

"Well, we better be on our way. Give our regards to Miley when he comes back!"

"We will and don't be worrying. It could be some other child. Goodnight to you's now and safe home."

Lassie got up and followed.

Patrick soon arrived home for the weekend. Mary asked him straight away.

"But what is this all about, Ma?"

She told him everything and showed him the medal.

"I'm not too sure what color I gave him. I had red and blue ones."

"But you did give him one?"

"Yes, I put it around his neck myself."

"I will have to go down to the station and let them know straight away."

"I will go with you and tell them that I am not sure about the color I gave him."

They went down and told the young Guard at the desk.

"Would you hold on here a minute, the Sergeant wants to speak to you."

"I wonder what he wants. They must have got some news."

"Here he is now, Ma."

"Hello, Mrs. Flynn. Thank you for calling in."

She went to hand him the medal. "You may hold on to that as our investigation is finished. It's bad news, I'm afraid. We strongly believe that it's your Son and you have our deepest sympathy.

Mary collapsed into Patrick's arms, roaring "My baby, my poor baby."

Two Guards came out and helped her into a chair. Her Son was crying as well. One Guard asked Patrick if he would be all right to go and get his Father.

"Yes, please look after Mam until I get back. I won't be that long. He's just having a pint."

He went to the pub and when his Dad and Joe set eyes on him they knew something was wrong. He told them the bad news and they went to the station.

"Are you sure, Guard?"

"Well, there is no other boy reported missing and the medical report shows that it is a young male about the same age as your Son. Where the body was recovered was only about twenty yards from where he disappeared."

News spread around the village and Father Tony

was the first to visit the cottage. Young Miley and his girlfriend had just arrived in the village. He was told the sad news. He went towards his Fathers place with tears running down his cheeks. When his Father seen him coming he went to meet them.

"What's wrong, Son?"

"It's Michael, Dad. They have found him. It is all around the village."

Maggie came out and was told the sad news too.

"Oh no, not poor Michael," she cried.

Dan sat beside the fire with his head in his hands, crying his eyes out. They were so shocked that Miley forgot about his girlfriend.

"Oh, sorry love, we don't even know your name," said Dan.

"Mam and Dad, this is Ann Cash."

"We are pleased to meet you. We have lost a good friend."

"That's all right. Miley has told me all about him. He was like a Brother to him."

"Right, Maggie," said Dan. "Let's get cleaned up and go and offer our sympathies to Seamus and Mary."

They all walked up the lonely road into the village and up to the cottage. Seamus opened the door and welcomed them in, even though it was a sad occasion. Mary tried to keep up her strength and was delighted to see Michael's old friends again. They wept with each other.

"He was going to be my best man but now he is gone," said Miley.

"Well, at least we can lay him to rest. We will never forget him. God rest his soul," said Mary.

Mary and Seamus went to Dublin. Joe and Sally went with them to take home their Son. When they arrived back into the village, there were crowds waiting near the crossroads. Dan and Miley helped them carry the coffin into the church, along with Joe and his Father.

The next day, he was laid to rest beside his Grandparents. David Byrne was watching from a distance and cycled away, alone in his thoughts. They all went back to the cottage and talked about the good times when Michael was there. Lassie never went into her basket after he left. She slept outside his bedroom door.

Miley went back down the country and was married the following year. Patrick was back in college and his mother only had Lassie for company during the day.

It was the start of the New Year when they found. David Byrne hanging from a tree. He had written a letter to Father Tony, which he wanted to be read at his funeral. In the letter, he told the truth. He admitted that it was he who had pushed James into the water. It was an accident and he said that he couldn't live with the guilt and humiliation he felt. He asked the Flynn family to forgive him for what he had done and anyone else he hurt. He was laid beside his friend James. Mary went through turmoil after the revelation. Her mind raced. It was a consolation to have her boy's name cleared at last. She would have liked Michael there to hear it though. Every Sunday after Mass she would place flowers on all of their graves. She did not feel ill towards David. They were all just kids and knew no better themselves.

Six months after David's funeral, his poor Father took a heart attack and died. He had a massive funeral and Molly sat beside his coffin in the church, even after all the grief she gave him in life. His wife moved out of the village and went back to her own friends to live.

Mary would take a walk up to see Sally and young Emma every day. That child put the spark back into her but Michael was in her thoughts every day. On the way back from Sally's one evening, she saw Dixie and he saw her.

"How are you, Son? It's been a long time since you were around this village."

"Sure they let me out Mrs. Flynn, but me Dad is still in there and he thinks he's the Pope."

"Why is that?" she asked.

"He's going around in there giving every one he meets his blessing. They are all stone mad in that place. One lad paid me sixpence a week to wash his bike."

"And did you do a good job on it?"

"Sure, he had no bike. It was all in his head."

She laughed.

"I miss your Son. He was a good friend but he's watching over us. We never did get that budgie to talk."

"Who?" she asked.

"Michael and the lads, we kidnapped him one night and the other lads wanted to kill him for not talking but Michael wouldn't let them. He brought it home and gave it back to her."

The little scamp, she thought to herself, no wonder the Midwife liked him.

"Are you back with your Mother?" she said out loud.

"Yes, I have to look after her. My Sister is gone."

"Where did she go?"

"Went off with some gobshite - to marry him, the fool."

He saw the Midwife coming up the hill.

"I better be off. The banshee is coming. Goodbye, Mrs. Flynn. I have to go. She is always hitting me with her blackthorn stick."

He was gone before she came up to Mary.

"How are you keeping, Mam?"

"Grand, Molly. I see you got a new pet. My girl must like her and she is a collie too."

"Aye, my poor Polly died. I had to get something to keep me company. It's a male. I was always looking at your young boy and his dog so I bought one the exact same and called him Jack after my Husband. He was a dog as well."

"God, he's beautiful, Molly. Sure, they are a grand breed of dog and very smart."

"Well, you want to watch your girl. Look down at him! He's getting a boner! I think I will have to get him castrated. He's like my Husband a dirty old bugger."

"Well, the best of luck with him, Molly. I have to get home and make the dinner." "Take care, Mam, it was nice talking to you. Goodbye now.

When Mary got home, she told Seamus about Molly's new dog.

"Her new pet, he's a twin of Lassie."

"Did you notice the way she cocks her ears every time we are talking?"

"Yeah, she knows everything we say. She is with us over ten years now."

The next morning when Seamus was gone to work, she started barking at the back door.

"What is wrong with you now?" asked Mary as she opened the door. Who was outside?

Only Jack.

"You better not let Molly catch you," said Mary as Lassie ran out to play with him.

"What are you doing up here at this hour of the morning? Oh, I see you are courting," said Mary to Lassie and Jack.

It was coming up to Christmas when Mary ran into Miley in the village with his Wife. They hugged each other and he told her that they now had a baby Son.

"That's great news."

"I am bringing him down to see you later on."

"Oh, that is lovely. What did you call him?"

"Michael, I hope you don't mind?"

"Course not, why should I? He would have loved that."

"Don't forget to bring down your parents and we can all have a little drink together." When they arrived at the cottage, Seamus was glad to see all of them again. They had a right good chat and Miley had a beautiful Son. They all loved him.

"You're a lucky man, Dan. We won't have any

Grandchildren now" said Seamus sadly. "I didn't think that Patrick would go to be a Priest."

"God, now I remember," exclaimed Mary. "Sure, it was Michael who told me that he would be a Priest and he was right."

"When was that?" asked Seamus.

"I don't know exactly. It was coming back from one of our trips I think."

"And I thought he would take a job in the mill and settle down with a girl."

"It was God's will. He lived in the church day and night. His old friend is not too well," said Mary. "Father O' Leary, he's bedridden and gone very feeble. But, he must be a good age."

"Well, we will be off before that child catches a cold. It is a good walk home. Happy Christmas to you and I hope you see many more."

"Many happy returns, Dan and don't forget to call again. I do be glad of the company."

Father O' Leary passed away in the New Year and Patrick came home for his funeral. It was a massive funeral and the Bishop helped say the Mass. They laid him to rest facing the church door, where he had spent many years. Patrick would be getting ordained this year and his Parents were very proud of him.

Patrick would now be twenty-two, and Michael would have been going on twenty-one.

Mary got up one morning and Lassie was after giving birth to six pups. She called Seamus and he did not know what was wrong.

"Would you look at this," she said. "Aren't they are lovely, I thought she was gone too old."

"Aye and I know who the Father is."

"Who?"

"Molly's dog. They have been courting a while."

"Well, the auld divil. What are we going to do with all of them?"

"I am keeping two of them and Joe can have one."

"Dan and Miley can have one each and that only leaves us with one left to give away." "God, you have it all worked out. I will tell Joe when I meet him this morning."

When he arrived home that evening, Joe came with him to see the pups.

"They are lovely, Mary. My Dad will take the last one and Emma will be delighted." "That settles it then. They are all going to good homes."

Lassie cocked her ears. In the meantime, Patrick was ordained and came back to his village for his first Mass. He gave his blessings to his Parents and to his

Godparents and to little Emma. When he got up in the pulpit, he gave a lovely sermon all about his life in the village. He talked about his brother and the tragedies that happened in their little village.

"I will be leaving here shortly and going to a new parish in a mining village in Wales. I hope and pray that we never have to go through this pain again. There are two of my best friends lying there in our graveyard, along with my Brother. Let's all forget the past and forgive each other's wrong doings. Let's live in peace."

The people stood up and gave him a standing ovation and clapped their hands. Dan and Maggie were outside when Mary and Seamus came out, standing at Michaels grave.

"That was a lovely sermon. We heard it from the back of the church. Why did you not come up to the altar, Dan?"

"We have always stayed at the back, Seamus."

"But why, Dan? You are one of us."

"A lot of those people wouldn't accept us."

"So that's the reason why you have always stayed outside, even when Miley got his communion."

"Yes, that's the reason."

Patrick joined them and he gave Dan and Maggie his blessings.

"Well, Dan, they are having a party for Patrick

in the school and it would be an honour if you and Maggie would join us."

"If Father Pat doesn't mind."

"Why should I mind, Dan? You were the best in the world to my Brother. You are the best friends we had during the trouble. You stood by us."

"All right then, let's go to the party."

They all walked in together. Mary told Dan about Lassie's pups and that she would like him and Miley to have one.

"That would be wonderful. I always thought the world of that dog, and she's so cute."

It was a wonderful party and when Patrick left for Wales, they knew that he would be missed. Mary was going to see young Emma and Lassie was behind her, with all her pups. She ran in to Molly on the way there.

"I told you he was a randy auld get."

"I am glad she had them," said Mary. "She's getting old herself."

"We are all going that way, love."

"I have to be going, Molly and get back in time to put on Seamus's dinner."

"Well, goodbye then love."

When she arrived at Sally's, young Emma was over the moon with all the pups. "Which one is mine, Aunty Mary?"

She always called her that and it made Mary happy.

"Whichever one you want love. Sure, pick out one and it can stay here with you."

She picked out her pup and Lassie returned home with five pups.

The next morning Mary received a letter stating that she was left a farm.

"How could that be so?"

She wrote back to the Solicitor to find out who had left her a farm. She showed her Husband the letter and he asked her if she knew who left the farm.

"God, it has me mystified. I wouldn't have a clue. All my relations have passed away."

"Well, you will just have to wait till he gets back in touch with you."

And that wasn't long coming, as the Solicitor called out to her cottage next day.

"It was an Aunt of yours who left you the farm in Scotland, your Mother's Sister."

"Oh, I never thought she had a Sister. It is the first time I heard of it."

"Well, it is true anyway and you are the only relation left so it is yours."

"And what am I going to do with a farm in Scotland? This is my home here."

"We can put it up for sale for you if you like. It will fetch a good price."

"Alright, go ahead then. I will leave you in charge of the sale."

"Right then, I will be going. I have a farm to sell. Goodbye and thank you."

Seamus was delighted when he was told the news. It was about time that they had a bit of luck.

"You are going to be a well off woman now, love."

"Ah, what good is it without my baby? We just have to carry on the best way we can but we will never forget him."

"I know that, love, but I keep wondering how did it happen to us?"

"It was God's will. Sure he has taken Patrick as well to look after his flock."

"Maybe something good will come out of all this in the end."

"I hope so love."

When Seamus had gone to work the next morning, Mary went up to see Emma and Sally. When Mary got home she put on Seamus's dinner and had everything ready. He was late, she thought. Maybe he had gone for a pint or called in to see Joe because he was off work sick. It was Dan that found him on the road while out collecting some sticks. He was unconscious. He got him up into the pony and trap and took him to the Doctor. He had collected Maggie on the way and told her to go and get Mary. When Mary answered the door Maggie was in a panic.

"Hurry up, Seamus has taken bad."

"What are you telling me? Slow down."

So she told her again and they rushed to the Doctor's house.

"How is he, Doctor?"

"He is very lucky to be alive. Only this man got him in time, he was gone. His heart is strained and too much pressure is bad for him. He can never work again. From now on he will have to take it easy and he will be fine. You can take him home now and put him to bed. I will call up tomorrow to check on him."

Dan put him back up on the pony and trap and brought them all home.

"Oh God, Dan, how can I ever thank you? Only for you, he was dead," she started to cry.

They put him to bed and she made them stay and have something to eat.

"That new Doctor is very nice. I don't know his name," said Dan.

"I will find out tomorrow," said Mary. "I will have to go up and tell Joe to let his boss know in the morning anyway."

"Do not worry about that, Mary. Stay here in case he wakes up. I will tell him on the way."

Just then Lassie walked over to him with her pups and started to lick him.

"God, you have a lovely family girl," he said as he petted her pups.

"How is Miley keeping, Dan?"

"He has another child on the way."

"That's great news! When you see him tell him that I was asking for him."

"You can tell him yourself. He will be down next weekend and he won't leave the village until he sees you. Well, we better be off. Goodnight, Mary."

"Thanks, Dan and you too, Maggie."

When they left she looked in on her Husband he was still asleep. There was a knock on the door. As she came out of her bedroom, she opened it. Joe stood there.

"How is he Mary?" asking anxiously.

"Asleep at the moment. Come in to the sitting room." She sighed. "He was very lucky, poor auld Dan was out collecting wood and he found him in time."

"And what did Doctor Blake tell you?"

"That he will never work again but I don't mind that."

"So that is the new Doctor's name. Will he be here in the morning to check on him?" "Yes, he will. Go in and see him now while I put on a nice cup of tea."

He got up and went to his room. When she had the tea ready she went in to call Joe, he was holding his hand and crying.

"Wake up my old friend. I will be lost without you and we're too long together." Mary put her hand on his shoulder.

"Come on, Joe and have some tea."

Before he left for home he told her that his Dad and Sally were going to call up to see him tomorrow.

"That will be grand, Joe."

"We are going to miss him at the mill. It will be dead without him."

"I will have to write a letter to Patrick tonight and let him know, them two were so close."

"I will see you, Mary. I will call in on my way home from work."

"Good night, Joe."

When he was gone she sat down and wrote a letter to her Son in Wales. She checked on Lassie and her pups, she was lying down out side Michael's door. She filled up a basin of water and left it at her side.

"You're still waiting for your Master!"

From the day he had disappeared Lassie still sat

there expecting him to come out the door. It was late when she decided to go to bed and the wind was howling outside. She heard a wailing noise.

"Oh my God, it's the banshee's death call."

She knelt down in front of the picture that her Son won at the carnival and prayed. It started to fade away now and she got into bed but could not sleep. She held her Husband and sat up all night.

"There's a death in the village," she said to herself.

She got up early next morning and had the cottage cleaned. There was a knock on the door. It was Doctor Blake.

"Good morning, Mrs. Flynn. How is our patient today?"

"He's still asleep. Come and I'll take you to his room."

She led the Doctor in. She was surprised when her Husband opened his eyes and asked how she was.

"You're ok. Thank God for that!" she said.

"You're a very lucky man," said the Doctor. "And as I told your Wife, your working days are over."

"Why, Doctor?"

"You've put a heavy strain on your heart. You may just slow down! Can you remember anything from yesterday?"

"Just closing the gates in the mill."

"Only that kind man found you in time, you would be wearing different clothes today." "Who was that? I would like to thank him."

"It was Dan, love. He was out collecting wood for the fire."

"God, I owe that man my life and when I'm able to get up, I'll look after him."

"Well, I will examine you now."

"I'll let you get on with it and I'll make you a cup of tea."

Mary went out and made the tea and brought the tray into the sitting room. She heard the Doctor telling her Husband to take it easy. Then he came to the sitting room.

"Sit down there and rest yourself," Mary said, handing him the tea and biscuits.

"I do feel really tired this morning. I had a late call last night. A poor old lady passed away."

"Did you know her?"

"Never met her in my life but I was told that she was a midwife here."

"Oh God, its poor old Molly Casey - a good friend, Doctor. God rest her soul. She was a great old character herself and poor old Doctor Byrne. I will miss her."

"I studied with Doctor Byrne. The poor old chap

was carrying too much weight and then his young Son committing suicide was a heavy blow to him."

"Yes, poor David. Sure, I lost my poor baby as well."

"Yes, I was told about the tragedies here. I am so sorry for you. I know what the pain is like and the heartache. I lost my good Wife but we have to just struggle on through all the turmoil. I was left with two sons to rear."

"What caused her death, Doctor?"

"She died of cancer. I felt relieved when she passed away. I watched her in so much pain and could do nothing to help her. She never complained."

"And your sons? Are they young?"

"They're teenagers now and a great comfort to me. I am so grateful to them. They were a tower of strength. I still think about her every day though. Do you know, Mrs. Flynn, it is hard enough to see someone old dying but a young person…"

"That must have broke your heart. I have seen Mothers who lost their child, myself included and it's heartbreaking."

"Well, I better be off, I'll call around again and keep an eye on him."

He got up to leave. Mary walked him to the door.

"Thank you for the tea. I really enjoyed our chat.

It's grand to have someone to talk to, who understands the pain and torment."

"Goodbye, Doctor and I will be looking forward to you coming again."

When he was gone, she thought what a nice man he was but still she thought of Molly. She made the breakfast and went in to her Husband.

"I'm glad you are going to be alright. You gave us such a scare."

"I will miss the lads at work. Now, what am I going to do all day? I have always worked."

"There is only the two of us now and when this farm is sold, we will be grand."

"I wish Dan would come in till I thank him, only for his firewood my goose was cooked."

"Poor auld Molly passed away last night. I heard the banshee wailing and I knew it was a death."

"Ah sure, she would have frightened the banshee. God, love, we are going to have two now."

"Two what?"

"Banshees of course."

"That is a terrible thing to say. She wasn't a bad person. She brought a bit of life to this village. She was afraid of no one."

"I wonder who will get her cottage and her money?"

"It is her poor dog that I am worried about."

CHAPTER TEN

That evening, Seamus had a house full of visitors all asking about his welfare.

"Mary, poor auld Molly is going to the church tomorrow night," said Sally.

"Yes, we will have to go and pay our respects. We are going to be lost without her." So they attended her funeral. She was buried the following day after Mass.

"Will you look at that Mary?" said Sally.

"What?"

"Where they buried her!"

"Sure, that's her Parents graves."

"I know that, but look at the other side."

"Oh holy God, the poor auld Doctor! He can't get away from her."

"There will be an underground movement there, if Molly has her way."

"Look over there, that's poor Dixie. I didn't think he would attend."

"There's Father Tony. I want to ask him about the poor auld dog."

Mary went over to him and asked about Molly's dog, Jack.

"He will be fine, Mrs. Flynn. Molly, she was a very clever woman."

"Why is that, Father?"

"She left everything to the church, on one condition."

"What was that?"

"The church has to look after her dog so I'm landed with a collie."

"That's great. You will have him for company and be able to take him for walks."

"She is the first woman that I know who outsmarted God himself."

Mary could only laugh as she walked out the gate with Sally. Dixie was waiting outside and came over to her.

"Who got her talking budgie?" he asked.

"The budgie died Dixie, died a long time back. Did you not know?"

"No, I did not. That is why I came to her funeral. Now they are both dead. Well, fuck it anyway!"

He went on home and was very disappointed that he didn't get her budgie.

When Mary got home, Father Pat was sitting down with his Father.

"When did you get in, love?" she asked as he came over to kiss her.

"I arrived this morning in Dublin. I am here for a few days just to see how Dad was faring out. Are you all right?"

"Yes, I am just coming back from Molly's funeral." Said Mary.

"Dad told me. God rest her soul. If I had arrived earlier, I would have attended her funeral. She was a great character."

"Father Tony was telling me she left everything to the church including her collie." "You're joking? God, she was a very smart woman. There was definitely no flies on her. Dad was telling me that only for Dan, he would not be around today."

"That's true, Son. We owe that man for your Father's life and for caring for Michael."

"Well, Mam, you can be sure that God will have a place for him in heaven. I want to try to do something here for him. The poor man never had much."

"How are you getting on in your new parish over in Wales?"

"Great, Mam, but there is a lot of poverty around that village and a lot of deaths." "How is that, Son?"

"The coalmines and the poor creatures are underpaid. I love listening to the choir over there. The Welsh are beautiful singers and lovely people."

"Well, I am going to take Lassie and the pups up to Dan. I promised him two," said Mary. "I will see you later. Watch your Dad and make sure he takes it easy."

She arrived at Dan's and Miley was home, he was overwhelmed to see her.

"I just came up with your pups. I know they will have a good home."

"How is Seamus keeping? Is he grand now?"

"Yes, thanks to you. He wants you to call in."

"I was just saying that to Maggie so we are going in this evening."

"And how are you keeping, Miley?"

"Grand, we have a baby girl now."

He let a shout at Ann to bring out the baby to show Mrs. Flynn. She was in feeding her. Ann came out and put the child into Mary's arms.

"She is beautiful, Miley. Have you picked a name for her?"

"Yes, I am going to name her after you, Mrs. Flynn."

"Ah thank you, Son."

"I would like if you and your Husband could be her Godparents."

"We'd be delighted, Miley. Wait till Seamus hears this, he'll be over the moon. I better be on my way. I will be looking forward to your visit tonight. Patrick is home."

"That is good. I am glad that you have him home for a couple of days."

The pups were getting upset when Mary went to leave them behind. Lassie walked back to them and gave them one last lick. They soon settled down and began to play. It was as if Lassie had told the pups that they had a good home there and would be looked after. Mary told Seamus that Dan and the family would be calling in that night. He was delighted.

"Patrick, get some money and go to Carpenters for me. I want a few drinks for our guests tonight."

"Here Son, a few pounds to go with your Father's."

She told him they were also celebrating being left a farm in Scotland and the possibility of its sale this week.

Dan and the family arrived that evening and they got a warm welcome from both Seamus and Father Pat. Father Pat thanked Dan.

"Only for you, we would not be having this party tonight. Thank you."

Later that night when Maggie was half pissed, Father Pat asked her to sing a song.

"Go on, love. Sing a song for this family."

"Get me another bottle and I'll sing all night."

She sang 'The whistling gypsy' and it brought tears to them all. It was Michael's song. "Dan, your woman is the best singer I heard in a long time. Michael was right."

After a few days, Father Pat had to return to Wales. They would all miss him. Seamus got better and he and Mary stood for young Miley's daughter. They all shared another good night together. Joe and Sally were also invited and they had great sport with young Emma. Miley decided to settle back down in his village to keep an eye on his Parents. Dan gave them the barrel wagon and he and Maggie took to the tent. They were sitting down around the fire one morning when Lassie appeared.

"God, look at this Maggie. The poor lass has come to see us. Ann, get her a bowl of water."

She drank the water and lay down beside Dan.

"God, you are getting auld, girl."

Her pups came over to her and she started licking them, one at a time. When she got up to leave, she could hardly walk.

"Miley, yolk up the pony and trap."

Lassie knew what he was after saying and sat down for a few minutes. When she got up, she went straight to Maggie and started to bark.

"What is the matter with you, poor girl? Dan is going to take you home."

She walked over to the pony and trap and looked back at Maggie. Dan lifted her up gently and Miley went with him into the village. When Mary seen them pull up outside the gate, she went out to meet them.

"Dan, I let her out for a few minutes and when I looked out again she was gone." "Yes, she came up the whole way to pay us a visit. Poor girl can hardly walk."

They lifted her down and she went back to Miley and barked at him. She done the exact same with Dan and looked back before she went in the door.

"I will have to get the Vet tomorrow to have a look at her. Thanks for bringing her back."

That night she just lay there with her two pups and wouldn't eat a thing.

"What is wrong with you girl?"

She just let a bark.

"I wonder if she is in pain," said Mary. "I will go

down early in the morning and get the vet to come up and have a look at her."

When they were going to bed that night, she got up and went to Mary.

"My poor girl, you are getting old. Lie down now and have a rest." She walked down and lay outside Michael's door with her two pups. Seamus got up the next morning and found her dead beside her pups. They were both heart broken and when Dan was told he also cried. They buried her in a corner in the back garden. They would never forget her loyalty.

The farm in Scotland was sold and it made a great price. They had no worries for the future. Mary went up to Dan and gave him enough money to buy two new wagons. Seamus spent his time around the garden and walking to the village with his Wife but every Saturday he went down to Carpenters to have a drink with Joe. They would play cards and have competitions throwing rings at the ring board.

One Saturday when he was in the pub, a knock came to her door. Mary thought it was Dan or Miley but when she opened the door it was a stranger.

"Good afternoon, Mam. I'm looking for the whereabouts of Seamus Flynn."

He had a strange voice, one she never heard before.

"He is not here at the moment. I am Mary Flynn if I can help you. What do you need my Husband for?"

"I am his Brother, John."

"God almighty, won't you please come in"?

She was excited as she led him into the sitting room.

"Sit down there and I will get you a bite to eat."

She put on the kettle and went back in to him.

"I am so glad I met you. Seamus never gave up talking about you."

"How is he keeping?"

So she sat down and told him the whole story of years gone by.

"God, you had a rough time. I sure would like to meet this Dan fella. And you tell me that you have a son a Priest over in Wales? That is great."

"And how about yourself? Are you married?"

"God, no! I was too busy making my fortune. I have great memories of this old cottage when Mam and Dad were alive. And you say he's out drinking with Joe? I sure would be glad to surprise them. Are Joe's Parents still alive? They were very good to us after our Parents died."

"Of course they are. Hold on till I change and I will go with you to Carpenter's. He is going to get the biggest surprise in his life when you walk in."

When they walked in through the doors of the pub, Seamus and Joe were up at the bar. They had their backs turned and did not see them coming up from behind.

"Are none of you guys going to buy an old friend a drink, after all these years?"

When Seamus looked around, he was shocked.

"God almighty, is it you John?"

"All in the flesh, little Brother."

They wrapped their arms around each other and the tears that fell would drown you. "Thanks, Joe, for keeping an eye on him."

"God, John, I'm going to get Mam and Dad."

"I told you, love, that I was going to meet him some day."

They got the drinks in and sat down to talk about old times. Joe arrived with his Parents and John stood up to greet them.

"Welcome home John. You're the best tonic we had around here for a long time."

"Well I am glad to be back on Irish soil. I am going to buy myself a little cottage here."

"There is one going here at the moment. It belonged to the Midwife."

"Was she a handsome woman? I don't want an ugly woman haunting the house."

"Oh yeah, John, she was a Film Star. It was a pity you didn't come back sooner, she was loaded."

"I sure missed out on that woman, I definitely should have come back sooner!"

When they got back home, they were up most of the night talking about the old days. Mary had a letter from her son on the Monday morning and it was good news.

"Seamus, your Son has become the new parish Priest in a place called Camberwell." "Where the hell is that place?"

"It's in London somewhere. Oh, I am glad for him."

"God, that is great news. Well, John, you have a Nephew a parish Priest now."

"It won't be too long more till we have a Pope in the family the way things are going." There was a knock on the door. It was Dan outside.

"How are you, Dan?" asked Seamus.

"Fine, just fine," he replied.

"Come on in. I want you to meet someone."

"Is that Dan I hear love?" asked Mary as they walked in. John stood up and Mary introduced him.

"It's a pleasure to meet you, Sir."

"The pleasure is all mine, Dan. I was looking forward to meeting you. Just call me John. I would like to thank you for saving my Brothers life. These people idolize you. Come and join us in a drink," he suggested as he poured a big glass of brandy. "I would like to make this toast to a good member of this family. To you, Dan," said John.

They had to lift Dan into the pony and trap that evening. It was the pony that took him home. Patrick would be thirty-two now and young Michael would be thirty-one this Christmas. It would be sixteen years that month since Michael disappeared. Time flies, Mary thought to herself.

Father Pat arrived in London by taxi. The house-keeper met him at the parochial house. Annie Fitzpatrick was her name, a big size woman with a great sense of humor. He knew that he would get on with her. Father Paul was then introduced to him. He had come from Holland. It was the first time Father Patrick had heard a Dutch accent and he was quite amused by it. Everyone was very nice and he soon settled in. He was up early the following morning and said first Mass. When Mass was over, he greeted his new congregation who seemed pleased with him. He was there about two weeks when Father Paul brought him over to the girl's school. He met a few Nuns and then asked about the where abouts of the Mother Superior.

"She is over in the hall, Father," replied one of

the Nuns. "We are decorating for Halloween. We have a little party for the girls before they break up for their holidays."

Both Priests entered the hall and there were lots of little girls running around. They were holding balloons, banners and masks and making a lot of noise. Father Patrick was approaching the Mother Superior when a little girl bumped into him.

"Sorry, Father," said the little girl.

Father Patrick thought she reminded him of someone but he was meeting so many people that he wouldn't have remembered, he just forgot. Sister Ann was delighted to meet him and they had a good old chat about things.

"Father, will you come to the dance on Saturday night? It would be a good opportunity to meet the children," she asked.

"I will," he said. "I'm looking forward to it already."

He then headed off on his rounds with Father Paul. First, he went to visit some of the old folks and then went on to the hospital to visit the sick. He went to the children's part of the hospital and had a good laugh with them. He was surprised to see that so many of them were terribly ill but could still share a smile. He was beginning to like it there already.

His next stop was to visit the Bishop, as he was away when he had first arrived. There, they ate dinner, had a chat about his travels and had a few drinks.

Halloween came and Father Pat headed off down to the School dance. He met Sister Ann inside the door. She grabbed an extra chair and they sat down. He could hear the music and the laughter coming from the bottom of the hall. It was obvious that the children were having a good time. Kids were running in and out to the toilets so Sister Ann went to see if everything was all right. She was only back about ten minutes when they could hear an awful commotion coming from the toilets. Both Sister Ann and Father Pat went to see what was going on. A fight had broken out. They were kicking and slapping at one another. There was a heap of them on the ground. Father Pat interceded and began pulling the boys up one by one.

He had them all up except for the boy who was face down on the floor. When he turned him over he got the fright of his life, so much of a fright that he ran out of the hall and home to the parochial house. Sister Ann was very shocked at his reaction and when the children had settled down, she followed him over to see what was the matter with him.

Annie, the housekeeper was still awake when Father Pat came home. Judging by the look on his face she could tell there was something wrong. She went to the cupboard to get him a brandy in the hope of settling him down.

"You look like you've seen a ghost, Father Pat," said Annie.

"I have," he said.

It was not long before Sister Ann arrived, followed by Father Paul and Father Hurley. They too noticed that Father Pat was not himself.

"Is it something you would like to talk about?" Asked Father Paul.

They all sat down at the table and Father Pat explained. He told them about his Brother Michael who disappeared nearly sixteen years ago and about the boy that was buried back home.

"In the hall," he said, "I could have sworn that the last little boy I picked up was my Brother."

Sister Ann rushed back to the hall but it was too late, everyone had gone home. Sister Ann told Father Pat that the boys were from St Peters and that she would inquire about that boy.

Father Pat woke early on Sunday, as he could not sleep thinking about the boy on the floor. He got up and said early Mass. It was later on that Sister Ann called to the house. She was talking to Sister Pious of St. Peter's School who promised to look into it. The boys would not be back from their holidays until

Monday week. Sister Ann told Father Pat that there were a few Flynn families attending that School. Father Pat thanked her for all her help and said he would call on Sister Pious after the holidays. It was a long week and Father Pat tried to keep himself occupied the best way he could.

Monday morning finally came and he decided to walk to the school. He had to cross from the girl's school. It was cold and he was glad he took his topcoat. He arrived there before the boys came and met with Sister Pious. She took him into her room and made him some tea. He could hear the children coming. They were all shouting and playing around with one another. He asked Sister Pious if she would go to each class looking for a boy with the Flynn surname. She went around each class and ended up with ten names. She collected those boys and sent them into Father Pat, one by one. It was the seventh boy who came into Father Pat that he recognized. He was the boy that he turned over on the floor. He was the image of his Brother. He was asked his name and he replied,

"Michael Flynn, Father."

Then he asked the boy where his Father originated from. The boy replied,

"Ireland."

He went out and told Sister Pious that this was

the boy he was looking for. The young boy asked if he was in trouble over the fight at the dance.

"No, Son," Father Pat said.

Father Pat took out a photograph from his pocket and showed it to the young boy.

"That's funny. My Dad has the same photograph as that. My Mammy found Daddy last Christmas crying with that photo."

Father Pat went on to question the boy. "What does your Father work at?"

"He's a Building Contractor. He even built the house that we are living in now."

He asked the boy if he would know the way home on his own.

"Yes," said the boy. "I only live on the other side of Camberwell green."

"Have you got any Brothers or Sisters?"

"Yes, I have two Sisters, Mary and Maggie. I have a younger Brother called Myles but we call him Miley. He's the baby."

"Would you know who I am?"

"The new Parish Priest," he replied. "My name is Father Patrick Flynn and I think your Dad is my long lost Brother. So that would make you my Nephew and me, your Uncle."

"Fuck me! I have an Uncle a Priest."

Father Pat laughed. He didn't mind the profanity.

He smiled at the child and thought of the similarity between him and his Father.

"I am not sure if we are related just yet. Did your Dad ever talk about Ireland?"

"Yes, he always talked about a little village at the foot of Mount Leinster in Co. Carlow."

Father Pat was amazed with what he just heard and began to realize his Brother was alive. He called out to Sister Pious and asked if he could take the boy out for the day.

"I will take him home as I am certain that this boy is my Nephew after all these years."

Sister Pious was delighted with the development and told the boy to collect his school bag. He returned with his school bag and walked out the door, saying goodbye to the Nun. They both were walking back towards the parochial house when the boy pointed at the school.

"That's where my Sister Mary goes to school." Then it came back to him. The little girl that ran into him was like his Mother's photo as a young girl.

When they entered the house all the Priests were delighted with the news. He showed the photograph and they all agreed that the boy was the image of his Brother. To be on the safe side Father Pat asked Father Paul for directions, but the young boy intervened.

"I know all of the green. I go with my Dad every Saturday around his building sites. To get to my house you have to take two buses but you will have to pay Father Pat coz I don't carry any money to school."

He was right they had to take two buses and then it took another ten minutes walk. At last they came to a long driveway and the boy pointed to the house in the distance. It took another ten minutes and then there were fifteen steps to the main door. Father Pat could not believe it as young Michael rang the doorbell. The housekeeper opened the door and was shocked to see Michael.

"You aren't in trouble again?"

"No he is not in trouble. I'm actually here to see his Mother and he kindly showed me the way. I am Father Pat, the new Parish Priest, dear."

"My name is Susan. I'm the Housekeeper. Well," she said, "Helen is actually in bed. She had a late night at a business function. Please come into the parlor. Michael, get Father Pat a drink while he's waiting."

"Some lemonade for me and a brandy for Father Pat," said the boy.

"How do you know that I drink?"

"Well, you wouldn't be a Flynn if you didn't."

Young Michael went to the drinks cabinet and took out the brandy. Once again he was cracking his Uncle with his jokes. He was a very funny child. His Father was the same and loved to have the craic with anyone.

"Michael," said Father Pat, "Don't say a thing about this until I talk to your Mother." Michael agreed. About fifteen minutes later, a beautiful woman walked through the door. She apologized straight away for making the Priest wait so long.

"That's all right, everyone deserves a lie in. We wouldn't be human otherwise."

The conversation started to stem and the lady went onto introduce herself.

"My name is Helen Flynn. I am very pleased to meet you, Father."

At this point the young boy was heading out the door when his Mother called him.

"Tell Susan to prepare breakfast for two. You will join me, Father. Won't you?" asked Helen.

"Yes, it would be a pleasure. It's not too often I get the chance to dine with such a beauty."

Over the breakfast table, the conversation stemmed even further.

"I don't think you are from England. Your accent is quite different."

He replied with a smirk, "With a name like Flynn, it's doubtful."

"God," replied Helen, "That's a coincidence! Our family name is Flynn too."

"No!" replied Father Pat, "It's not!"

He placed his hand in his pocket and took out a photo. He handed her the photograph and she looked at it in pure disbelief.

"How can this be? My Husband has the exact same photograph."

She then went to the cabinet and took out the photograph.

"Have a look at this."

"That's the same photograph that was taken on our Communion Day."

"What does this mean?"

"It means that the other guy in the photo is me. I'm his Brother."

She sat there in shock for a few moments then she began to smile and say.

"I knew that there was something wrong with his upbringing. I'm really glad he's not an orphan."

She got up to hug and kiss him repeatedly.

"I always thought the other boy in the photo was a child he met in the industrial school."

"I don't follow. What industrial School?"

"Well," said Helen, "He had just escaped from an industrial School when we met at the boat. Mum. had just buried her Mother and we were heading back to England. He helped Mum with the suitcases because she had three kids and was struggling. That is how he entered the boat and Mum befriended him. He told her he had escaped and that he was beaten every day and was only half fed. When we arrived in England, Mum reared him and I eventually married him. If you're his Brother that would explain why each Christmas he gets depressed. I would often find him crying with that photograph in his hand. Were you there too?"

"No," he replied. "He always had a good imagination when it came to stories. We lived with both Parents growing up. He disappeared one day and never came back. He was only fourteen and when they found a body, we all thought it was his."

"Yes, he was about that age when Mum met him on the boat and they all think he is dead?"

Father Pat went on to tell the story about Michael's disappearance and how he had found him. They talked until lunchtime and Susan came in. She had a pot of tea and some freshly made sandwiches. Helen introduced Father Pat but this time by breaking the good news that he was really Michael's brother.

Time passed quickly and it was almost time for Helen to collect her other children from school. She excused herself and left Father Pat in the safe hands of Susan and young Michael. Before she left, he asked her if he could use her phone, as he wanted to ring the house. Father Paul answered the call and was delighted to hear the good news.

It was a while before Helen returned but young Michael kept him amused. Father Pat told his Nephew all about Ireland and his Grandparents and the village life. Young Michael in return filled in all the blanks about his Dad and their current life.

Helen arrived home with the rest of her children and they were all introduced to Father Pat.

"How are you Mary?" asked Father Pat.

"I am fine, Father and thank you for asking."

She remembered him but was confused as to how he knew her name. Mary approached her Mother as she was coming in with youngest little boy.

"Mam, how did the Priest know my name?"

"He is your Uncle so he's bound to know you."

"I thought Daddy had no Brothers?"

"We all thought that," replied her Mother. "Do you remember your Daddy's most precious photograph?"

"Yes," she replied.

"Well, Father Pat is the other boy in it."

She was delighted and ran over and gave him a big hug. Helen went into the kitchen to talk to Susan while she was preparing the dinner. She could hear all the children questioning him about Ireland.

"Oh, you'll see it shortly, I promise you."

"When Father, when?" shouted the children.

He told them they would get to see Ireland and said Christmas would be a lovely time. Helen took all the children into the dining room for their dinner. She came back into Father Pat to talk to him.

"You must be exhausted," she said. "Children can tire you out."

"No," he replied. "They have made me the happiest man on earth. You know, I'd love to take you all to Ireland for Christmas," he proposed.

"I think that is a great idea. I hope your Brother feels the same."

They had another brandy and she sat and listened to Father Pat talk about the old days. The place was quiet as the children were in their playroom down the hall. They heard the noise of an engine in the driveway. She gasped with excitement.

"He's home."

CHAPTER ELEVEN

Father Pat did not know how to react although his body was shaking from head to toe. It would be a shock for Michael but Father Pat hoped that he would be glad to see him. Helen went out to greet her Husband and he remained in the sitting room. "We have a visitor," she said as she led her Husband into the room. He sat with his back facing the door and Michael wondered who this man could be. He turned to face him and rose quite quickly. With his voice shaking, he approached him.

"You've have changed a lot, Michael Flynn."

He wrapped his arms tightly around his little Brother and they both began to cry. Michael was in deep shock. But how?…when?…was all he could mutter. After a few minutes of cuddling, Michael took a deep breath and began to talk. His mind was racing.

"How did you find me? Are Ma and Da still alive?"

The questions were coming at Father Pat so quickly that he didn't have time to answer them.

"I am glad I found you. We have a lot to talk about."

Helen filled out two glasses of brandy. They were alone now as Helen was putting the children to bed.

"I always knew that you would become a Priest. I even made a bet with Mam. Remember St. Patrick?"

They both began to laugh. They had got the old times back. Michael wanted to know everything. He wanted to know about his Parents and who had passed away in the village.

He assured him that his parents were in good health, but broke the news about David.

"He hung himself but he had cleared your name and now everyone knows the truth."

He also told him about David's father and the Midwife, and about Lassie.

"God, I loved that dog. I knew that I would never see her again."

"But she had six pups and when you were gone, she slept outside your bedroom door. After you disappeared, Mam would not believe you drowned until a body was recovered."

"What body?"

"They pulled the body of a young boy, your age, out of the river and it took the Guards a month to investigate. They assumed it had to be you. They brought back the body from Dublin and the whole village attended your funeral. Mam, Dad and I accepted it was you until I discovered your Son. Poor Dan and his family were broken hearted and he saved Dad's life."

"I would love to see them again. How is Miley keeping?"

"He is great but he left the village. Why did you fake your own death?"

"I was scared after what Dan said. He told Miley all about the industrial Schools and what they were like. Dan was reared in one and that is why Miley never got into trouble. The whole village was against me and I knew I never stood a chance. I had saved money from the fruit picking so I planned an escape."

"Do you know that Mam and Dad never celebrated Christmas since you left home? Will you come this Christmas? I told Helen and the kids that they could."

"I wanted to sell up a long time ago and go home but I never had the guts. I am a millionaire, Pat, but I was never happy here in this country."

"Come home then. Mam and Dad are not going

to live forever. Dad had to retire with a strain on the heart."

"All right then. It will be a lot easier now that you have found me."

"You know that you just can't walk back in, I will have to go home and clear this all up. I will have to notify the Guards and then I will have to break the news to Mam and Dad. I will have to visit the Bishop tomorrow to get permission to travel home but I have to do one thing. I have to take your son with me so you will have to come home."

"That's ok; there will be no escaping for me then."

So it was all agreed.

Helen came back into the room and asked them if everything was all right.

"Yes, love. I have decided to move back to my home to Ireland."

"Oh, I am so glad."

"It was Helen and the children that kept me going all these years, only for her, I was lost. She is a good Wife, just like Mam, gentle and kind."

With that Helen asked Father Pat if he would stay the night as there was plenty of room.

"Yes, I would love to but I would have to make one more phone call back to the house.

The other Priests and the Housekeeper might get worried about me."

So they spent the night drinking and talking about old times gone by.

Susan arrived the next morning and let herself in when she went into the sitting room. She had seen Father Pat's topcoat and knew that he had stayed the night. She picked up the empty glasses and half eaten sandwiches and went to the kitchen. She also knew that Michael was not at work as his car was in the driveway. When she went to the kid's room, they were asleep. No school today! She smirked to herself. It was near the end of November and the weather was bitter cold. She began to make breakfast. She knew they would all need it upon awaking. Susan heard noises coming from the children's room and knew they were awake already. They all soon rushed into the kitchen asking if Father Pat was still there. They were delighted when they heard he was.

She began laying the table for the children. Father Pat came in and then greeted the children. She knew it was black coffee he needed most. Judging by the looks of him he must have had a skinful the previous night.

"God, you look like you over done it. That's what you get for drinking all night."

"I know but I am paying for it now. My head is bouncing."

"Well, drink your coffee and take these painkillers. They'll relieve your headache."

Soon after breakfast was made, Father Pat's headache eased.

"Michael, how would you like to come to Ireland with me?"

He was thrilled and started running around saying, "I am going to Mount Leinster." Susan then began to ask Father Pat about the rest of the family's position.

"I think my Brother and Helen are selling up completely and moving home."

That really shook her as she had been with this family a long time. They had always been generous with the wages as she had ten children to feed. She explained to him that her Husband was ill and he could only work the odd time.

"If I lose this job, it is going to be a real struggle for them."

Father Pat assured her that whatever happened, God would always provide for her and the kids. His Brother and his Wife arrived in the dining room and both of them had very sore heads. Susan poured out two black coffees for them and fetched more painkillers.

"How is your head today, Brother?"

"Not too bad but I better sober up before I see the Bishop."

They all laughed, holding their heads as Susan went off to the rooms to tidy up. She was trying to avoid Helen and Michael as she was sad and could not hide it. Helen noticed her weird behavior and asked her Husband if he did.

"God, I forgot about the hard work that she put into this family over the years. She was not only a Housekeeper but she has also been a family friend. I had not considered her when I made the plans to move back home."

He adored Susan and her family and upon consultation with his Wife, he decided to leave his mansion to her.

"It is too big for us anyway. It will suit her large family."

That afternoon as she was preparing lunch they asked her to sit with them for a moment.

"We have something to tell you."

"I know. You are leaving here for good and I will miss you."

"We will all miss you as you were always part of this family. We have decided to leave you this house and enough money to keep you going. It is a gift to you for caring for this family over the years."

She started to cry, as she could not believe it. Now her Husband could take it easy at home.

"Oh God, thank you. You have always been so kind to my family."

At that moment they all made a pact that they would keep in contact with one another. "Oh, I am missing you already, but I promise I will go to Ireland to visit you."

They all sat down to a lovely lunch. The atmosphere was one of great excitement. She told them that she was going in to church on the way home from work.

"I am going to thank God for such lovely friends and your kind offering."

"Well, I better go and see the Bishop or Michael or I can't go anywhere," said Father Pat, turning to Michael. "Come with me and the two of us can sort out everything."

"I have to go to the office anyway," said Michael.

They both went out the door and their first stop was to the building site.

"It's a bit mucky in here this time of the year so watch your step." Advised Michael.

When they entered the office, there was a colored man behind the desk.

"Ah, good morning, boss. How are you feeling today, man?"

"I am on top of the world this morning, John.

This man here is my brother. Patrick, let me introduce to you my very best friend and my top man,
Jamaican John."

"I am very pleased to meet you, man. You never
told me you had a brother, man."

"It's a long story, John. I will tell you all about it
before I leave. Take off your topcoat, Patrick and
hang it up there on one of those hooks."

When he took his coat off, John discovered that
he was a Priest.

"Man, you never told me he was a priest. Forgive
me, Father."

"That's all right, John. Sure there is nothing to
forgive."

"Would you like a nice cup of tea? It will warm
you up. It's freezing outside."

"Yes, that would be grand, John. Thank you very
much."

He went out the door and Patrick sat down beside
his Brother.

"He is a very pleasant man. How long have you
known him?"

"Since I arrived here. He is the same age as myself
and a great worker. God, I just thought of something. Remember Poor Dixie and the day at the
missions," said Michael, "What he said about the
black babies."

"Still, it's always talked about back home."

"It's a pity they took the poor chap into the mental. I must call in to see him."

"There is no need to. They let him out to look after his Mother. Mam was talking to him at Molly's funeral but he was in very bad form."

"I did not think he would attend her funeral. Coz, she used to hit him."

"He only went to find out who got the budgie but when Mam told him it died. He was sad."

"I have a great idea. I owe that chap a lot, all the times I fooled him."

"And what is your great idea?"

"To bring him home the parrot I keep in the garage. I have him a few years but I can't leave him inside the house, he would drive you mad."

"Ah, he would love that but why give him away now?"

"Well, if you had him up on the pulpit with you during Mass, your church would be empty. When I had him in the house, the language out of him was really bad, cursing all the time. They pick up everything you say and on account of the children, I had to put him in the shed."

Their next stop was to see the Bishop to tell him the story. Father Pat got consent to travel and the

Bishop was delighted for him. They then headed back to Michael's house where they remained for the rest of the night.

The next morning arrived and Father Pat prepared himself to leave and Little Michael had a lie in to prepare himself for the journey. It was time to go and Fr Pat said goodbye to Helen and the children. Michael drove them to Kings Cross Station. The train was ready to pull out for Holyhead.

"Goodbye, Dad."

"Goodbye, Son. Have a good time and behave yourself for Uncle Pat."

"I will, Dad. Don't worry."

Michael then handed Pat an envelope.

"Just a few pounds to see you through until I get home."

"Thanks, Brother."

They waved back at Michael as the train started to move. Little Michael was very excited and was really looking forward to the journey. They both reached Holyhead at two thirty and were then informed that their ship would be sailing at three o'clock. It was a beautiful afternoon, so when the ship began to sail Pat took little Michael up on deck. He really enjoyed looking out at the big blue ocean and could not believe the size of the ship.

"Come on and we will go get something to eat."

Even over lunch, little Michael was still inquisitive.

"When will we reach your village, Uncle Pat?"

"We will be off the ship by seven o'clock this evening and then we will get the last bus at seven thirty. We should be in the village by nine o'clock, if your patience can stick it that long. You will probably be dead tired by then though."

"No, I won't, Uncle Pat. Sure, I stayed in bed most of the morning."

Father Pat opened the envelope that his brother had given him and inside was three hundred pounds.

"Come on, Michael. We will go and have a look in the duty free section. I'd like to get a few presents for everyone back at home."

Little Michael was amazed at the things in the duty free and was delighted to be able to help his Uncle in choosing the presents. Father Pat was buying everything he laid his eyes on.

"How will we manage to carry all of this stuff, Uncle Pat?"

"Don't worry, son. We will get it home, no bother."

The ship was great but they were now on the bus

heading for the village. It was dark and Michael was a bit disappointed that he couldn't see anything. Father Pat assured him that there would be plenty of other opportunities to sightsee. At last they arrived in the little village. Father Pat told Michael that their first stop would be to the pub because that's where his Dad would be. They opened the door of the pub and went straight into the snug.

"What would you like to drink, Michael?"

"A coke, please, Uncle Pat."

"Well, sit down there and I'll ring the bell."

He rang the bell and out came Pat Carpenter. He was surprised to see him.

"Congratulations, I hear you're the new Parish Priest in London."

"Thanks, Pat. Could I have a coke and a brandy please?"

"They're on the house. Your Dad and uncle are inside as well."

"Uncle?" asked Father Pat. "Oh, I forgot, Pat. Sure, you wouldn't have known. Your Uncle from America is home. Your Dad is as happy as Larry."

"Don't tell them that I'm here. I'd prefer to surprise them."

"I see you have a little visitor with you," Pat Carpenter said, wondering who the little boy was. Father Pat just passed it off by saying that he was part of the surprise. When Pat Carpenter brought over the drinks to them he asked little Michael how he was.

"Very well," he replied with a strong cockney accent.

Pat Carpenter inquired further. "With an accent like that he can't be Irish."

"No," replied Father Pat, "but his Father is."

"Who would that be then?"

"I might as well tell you as it will be all round the village soon. He is my Nephew, Michael Flynn."

"But how, Father Pat? Sure, there's only yourself and Michael. God rest his soul." "Michael is alive, Pat and this lad here is his oldest Son."

"God almighty, you're right. He even looks like him when he was younger but who is the young lad buried in the graveyard then?"

"I don't know, Pat. I have to let the Guards know. I'll do that later when Mam and Dad know."

Pat had to sit down with shock.

"I'll tell you the whole story when I get time."

"God, it's a miracle. I can't believe it! The drinks are all on the house tonight."

"Now don't say anything to anyone till I tell me Parents."

"No, I won't. Go on in and tell your father and I'll keep an eye on this little fella."

His father spotted Father Pat as he came in the door.

"Well, would you look who's here, John. It's your Nephew."

Seamus got up to greet him. "How are you Son? What brings you home this time of year?"

I've some good news for you, Da."

"What a coincidence as I have some for you as well. Come up here and meet your Uncle John."

John stood up to greet his Nephew. Holding out his hand, he told Father Pat that he was delighted to meet him.

"And I'm pleased to meet you at last too. You put a bit of a spark in my Da," said Father Pat said as he shook hands with him.

"What will you have, Father?"

"Just call me Pat. I'd love a brandy, please."

"And what are you having, Seamus?"

"The same, John. Thanks."

John made his way to the counter and Seamus asked if Father Pat had seen his Mother yet.

"No, I just got off the bus and came straight here."

"Well, what's the good news that you have for me, Son?"

"Da, it's going to be a bit of a shock. There's a reason why I've come home."

"Well, don't keep me in suspense. Tell me."

"Michael is alive, Da."

Seamus just stared into space and couldn't speak.

"Are you alright, Da?"

"Are you sure, Son? How do you know?"

"I found him in London. He was living in my parish."

"Oh, holy Mother of God, why didn't you let us know? Who is the poor boy in the graveyard then Pat?"

"I don't know Da but it's definitely not Michael."

John came back with the drinks and felt that there was something wrong with his Brother.

"What's up Seamus? You look like you have just seen a ghost."

"My Son Michael is alive. Patrick has just told me."

"Well, that's fabulous news. Is it true, Pat?"

"Yes, I have been staying with him for the last week."

"How does he look? What has he being doing all these years?"

"He's the same old Michael. He's a millionaire now though and has four beautiful children."

"Why won't he come home, Son?"

"He's coming home next week, Da."

"I wouldn't be so sure," said Seamus, hanging down his head, depressed.

"He will be home, Da, I promise and just to make sure he would, I took his eldest Son home with me."

Seamus started to cry. He was going through all kinds of emotions.

"Don't cry, Da. I'll tell you the whole story tonight."

"I want to see my grandson, Pat. Where is he?"

"He's in the snug. I'll go and get him."

After a few minutes the door creaked back open and a little boy appeared. Seamus could not believe what he was seeing and couldn't take his eyes off him.

His mind was racing. It was real as he was the spit of his father. Seamus stood up as Pat directed the boy towards him.

"This is your Grandfather, Michael."

"I'm pleased to meet you, Grandfather."

Seamus lifted him up, bad heart or not and the tears just kept coming. He couldn't contain himself. He started hugging and kissing the child and eventually let him down after a long time.

"Why are you crying, Granddad? Aren't you pleased to see me?"

"Oh, of course I'm pleased. I'm crying with happiness."

He sat little Michael on his knee and told him

that he was the happiest man in the world. Once again Seamus hugged and kissed the child. Little Michael had never got so many hugs and kisses all at once before. Little Michael was already feeling a strong bond with his grandfather and he just knew that he would always love this old man.

"I love you, Granddad."

"I love you too and just wait till your Nan sees you. She'll be over the moon."

Joe then came in the door and was wondering what was happening. He approached Father Pat and asked him why Seamus was crying and about the young boy on his knee.

"It's his Grandson, Joe. Michael's alive and well."

"But how can that be?"

"It's a long story. Look at the boy closely enough and you'll understand."

Joe went over to his friend Seamus.

"It's a miracle, Seamus. He's the image of Michael."

Seamus introduced the child to his best friend.

"I better go and break the news to Mam," said Father Pat. Joe. "Will you ask Pat to mind the stuff that I left in the snug?"

"I will indeed, Father."

"Will you be okay with your Grandfather, Michael?"

"Yes, I'll be fine. I'm home to mind him for Dad."
They both hugged again.

"Da, will he be ok with you till I bring Mam down?"

"Of course, Son. What I have here, I will never let go."

Joe left the pub after Father Pat as he had to tell his family as well. His Parents were Michael's Godparents so they too would be anxious to know. Fr Pat went to the cottage and opened the door. Mary heard the door open and close so she got up. She just presumed that Seamus was home early. She was delighted to see it was Pat and went over to him and gave him a hug and kiss.

"What has you home so soon, love? You're not long gone back. Is there something the matter?"

"No, Ma. I have good news for you although it may come as a bit of a shock."

"Well, Son, I've news for you too. Your uncle John is home from America and he's the best tonic your Dad has had in years. How do you like being a Parish Priest? I'm really happy for you."

"I love it, Ma."

"Now you sit yourself down and I'll make you something nice to eat."

"Ma, just sit down for a minute. I want to tell you something."

"What, Son?"

"You'll be shocked when I tell you this but it is the truth. I have found Michael. He's alive."

"Oh my goodness and you are positive, Son?"

"Of course, Ma. I've seen him. He's living in London."

She started to cry and when she contained her emotions the questions started to come.

"Where is he? Is he all right? Is he coming home?"

She was delighted to hear he was doing so well but felt a bit upset that he hadn't made contact.

"Don't be upset, Ma. He'll be home next week and you can find out everything off him."

"Why did he not travel with you, love?"

"He's a millionaire, Ma and he had to stay behind to sell his businesses and arrange everything else."

"So he's coming home for good?"

"Yes, Ma. Isn't that great?"

"Oh love, I don't know what to think. You have me all confused."

"Well then, let me put your mind at rest. We'll go down to Carpenter's to Da."

She got her coat and off they went. They soon arrived in Carpenter's and when they approached the table that Seamus was sitting at Mary stopped.

She just kept looking at the little boy and it wasn't long till the pieces of the jigsaw started to fit together. Nobody had to tell her who this little boy was. It was a mother's instinct and she knew. The tears began to roll down her cheeks and she began to smile in amazement. Then she thanked the good Lord up above. She knew all her prayers weren't left unanswered. Little Michael asked his Grandfather if she was his Grandmother. Seamus confirmed that she was and then told him to go to her. Mary opened out her arms and little Michael ran to her. He threw his arms around her as she held onto him very tightly.

"I love you, Nan."

"Oh, I love you too, sweetheart," she said while kissing his cheek.

"Come on, let's go to Granddad," little Michael suggested. Little Michael caught her by the hand and took her the rest of the way over to Seamus. Seamus got up and the two of them fell into each other's arms crying as little Michael looked on. Mary was a little weak after the shock so everyone sat down. Little Michael sat in between Mary and Seamus, holding onto his Nanny's hand once again.

"I'll go and tell the Guards now, Ma," said Father Pat.

"Oh, I'm so happy, Pat. Thank you very much for finding him."

"We're all happy, Ma. I'll tell you the whole story tonight."

Off he went to the Garda station.

CHAPTER TWELVE

Pat Carpenter was handing the drinks to everyone who came in.

"What's the big occasion, Pat?"

"Over there in the corner. Michael Flynn is alive."

Joe, Sally and Emma came in and they all hugged Mary and little Michael. Everyone in the pub was elated. It was all around the village in a flash and that evening, every neighbour knew.

"God, Seamus, it's a pity that Maggie isn't here. She'd get the place going with a few sing songs," said Mary.

With that little Michael stood up and told his Grandparents that he wanted to sing the song that his Dad used to sing at Christmas when he got depressed. When Joe heard the little lad say that, he stood up and asked everyone in the pub to stay quiet for a few minutes. You could have heard a pin drop. The little boy told everyone that it was dedicated to his Grandparents who he had only met for the first time. Everyone clapped and Danny Halton went up and stood beside him with an accordion.

"Ready?" Asked Danny. "What are you going to sing?"

Michael bent over and whispered into his ear, 'The Whistling Gypsy.' He began to sing and everyone was amazed. Mary began to cry harder now and her tears wouldn't stop coming. Father Pat came back half way through the song and he just stood in amazement. He was such a talented little young lad with a great voice. Towards the end of the song everyone joined in even Mary, although she was fighting back the tears. When he finished, everyone cheered and clapped him. He loved the amount of attention he was getting.

He went back over to his Grandparents and sat back down in between them. He turned to them and asked if they liked it. They assured him that they did and told him about the lady who originally sang it.

"Wait till I tell Maggie. She'll be very pleased with you," said Mary.

Father Pat even suggested that he think about taking singing seriously as a career. They had a lovely evening in the pub and when they got back to the house, little Michael was delighted with Lassie's two pups. Mary knew the little lad was tired so she got the key for Michael's room and led him into it. He noticed an unwrapped present and quizzed his Grandmother about it.

"It is a bike I bought for your Dad many years ago but he never got to see it. You can have it now if you like, love."

"Yes, Nan, I'd love to have it. I can go and see all the different places on it. Thanks, Nan. You're the best."

"You have a good sleep, darling and I will see you in the morning."

"Goodnight, Nan."

She kissed him on the forehead and left the room. They both knew the full story that night, Father Pat told them everything and it was now beginning to sink in for them. The Guards were re-opening the case but even they were delighted with the news.

Mary found it hard to sleep that night, as she was afraid that she'd wake up and it would only be a dream. She checked on little Michael almost every hour during the night and every hour he was still there. It wasn't a dream but it could take some getting used to after years of grieving for a Son who had never died.

Little Michael was up early next morning playing with the two pups when Seamus came down.

"After breakfast, how about you and me go off for a walk?" suggested Seamus.

"Yes, Granddad, but where are we going?"

"We will go to the woods to get a Christmas tree and some holly so we can have the place ready for your Dad."

"Great, Granddad. Can I help you decorate the house?"

"Of course you can, Son."

After breakfast the two of them set off together. Walking through the village proved impossible as everyone was stopping Seamus, shaking his hand and congratulating him.

Further up the village, he spotted Miley heading towards him on the pony and trap. Seamus shouted,

"Miley, Miley! Come here!"

Miley pulled up alongside him and was wondering who the young boy was.

"How are you, Mr. Flynn?"

"Did you hear the news?"

"What news?" asked Miley as he got down from the pony and trap.

"Michael is alive in London. This is his Son Michael. He will be home next week." Miley stood there shocked and shaking.

"But how? It's not possible."

"It's a long story, son. Bring your family to the house as soon as you can and I will explain the lot."

Young Michael asked if he could get a spin on the pony and trap as he had never been on one before. Miley helped him up and he was delighted. Miley dropped them both up to the woods and he headed home to tell his Parents very excited.

As they were walking through the woods, Seamus told him about all the adventures that his Dad used to get up to in the woods and that he used to collect the holly and tree there too, when he was small.

"We're going to have a great Christmas, Granddad."

"That's for sure, Son."

Little Michael picked out the best tree and there was plenty of holly to gather. They gathered as much as they could manage to carry and headed home. As they were coming out of the woods, the bold Dixie was going in.

"Would you look who it is, Son?"

"Who?"

"That's Dixie. He used to be a great friend of your Dad."

Michael threw down his holly and ran to meet him.

"How are you, Dixie?"

Dixie was a bit confused and thought it was a ghost he was seeing.

"Is that you, Michael?"

"Yeah, it's me," laughed the little lad.

"But they buried you in the graveyard. How did you manage to get out of the ground?" "No, Dixie. I'm Michael junior."

Seamus intervened and explained to Dixie as best he could. Dixie finally realized what Seamus was talking about and was over the moon.

"Mr. Flynn, you're not allowed to be carrying anything heavy. Mrs. Flynn told me so give me that tree and I'll bring it home for you. I can get me own wood later."

You would swear that Little Michael knew Dixie all his life as they were talking and joking the whole way home.

Mary and Father Pat were up, but they were wondering where Seamus and little Michael had got to. Not long after they heard a noise outside. Mary opened the door and asked Dixie to come in for a bite to eat. She took Dixie inside and Father Pat was coming out of the sitting room.

"How are you keeping, Dixie?"

"Hello, Father Pat. They told me Michael is alive."

"Yes, he will be home next week."

"He'll be home for my birthday. It's next week too."

"Is that right?"

"Yes, Mrs. Flynn. I think I'm twenty one."

"You're more than that," said Father Pat. "Coz, me and you went to school together and I'm thirty two in March."

"Well, I must be the same age as you then. I don't really know because I never had a birthday."

Mary felt sad for him. Mary called Father Pat into the kitchen and Dixie stayed chatting to little Michael.

"What is it, Ma?"

"When you're going to see Father Tony, will you find out when Dixie was born? They will have it on record in the church."

"I sure will, Ma. I'm going up there now."

As he was going out the door, Dan, Maggie and Miley and the rest of the family were arriving. Father Pat told them to go on in and Mary would tell them everything.

When Father Pat told Father Tony about finding Michael, he was delighted for him and the family.

"How are you's all going to manage for room when Michael arrives?"

"Oh, we never thought of that."

Father Tony went over to the cabinet and took out the keys to Molly's cottage.

"Here, Pat. It's not for sale till the end of January. Michael can have it while he's here."

"That's very good of you. Thanks very much."

"And if you like, you can stay here."

"Yes I'd like that. It'd give you a break and I could say first Mass on Sunday for you."

"That'd be grand. I'm waiting on his Grace to send me a new Curate, but that won't be till the New Year."

"Could you do me another big favour?"

"If it's in my power, I will"

"I'd like to know Dixie's date of birth. He had to be born the same time as myself coz we were in infant School together."

"Come on then and we'll have a look."

"Richard Walsh would be his real name coz Dixie is only a nickname."

After a while, they discovered his records, he was born on the 21st of December.

"Oh-, that's Michael's birthday too and he's arriving that day. Mam will be delighted when she hears this. I will see you later on. Call up to the cottage for a drink."

When he arrived home, everyone was there helping to put up the Christmas tree and decorations.

"Look, Uncle Pat, Emma wrote out this to hang on the wall. What does it say?"

"It says 'Welcome Home, Michael'. Now isn't that nice?"

Dixie was still there helping Miley's children decorate the tree. Seamus and John were enjoying the company; they were like two kids themselves. He went into the sitting room where Dan, Maggie and Miley were having a drink.

"Ah, Father, sit down here and have a drink with us. It's brilliant news," said Dan.

"I suppose I will. It's quieter in here. There's chaos out there."

After his drink, Father Pat asked everyone if they could gather together as he had an announcement to make.

"Settle down now lads, I want to say something."

He told them that they had all done a splendid job and that the house looked great.

"Now, Father Tony has given me the keys to Molly's house so we will have to get it ready for Michael,

Helen and the kids. We won't have enough room here for them all."

"God, now we are going to have to get another Christmas tree and holly."

The kids were delighted that there was more decorating to be done and Father Pat gave his father the keys. Dixie suggested that he'd get the other tree and holly and Mary was delighted with the offer. Little Michael wanted to go with him, as he seemed to enjoy Dixie's company. His grandparents agreed and off they went together. Mary asked Father Pat if he found out when Dixie's birthday was.

"He was born on the 21st of December, the day Michael comes home."

"Sure it's Michael's birthday as well. We'll make it extra special."

Mary told the children to go down and make a start on Molly's house, as Dixie and Michael would be back with the tree and holly soon. Emma got the keys off Seamus and took all the children and Miley's Wife with her down to Molly's house. When the rest of the people had gathered in the sitting room, Mary stood up.

"I want to tell you's all something."

"What is it, love?" asked Seamus.

"It's about Dixie. I've just found out that his birthday falls on the same day as Michael's and that's the day he comes home. The poor auld chap has never had a birthday in his life. He's a harmless auld divil so I'm going to buy him a big cake and candles. Michael and Miley here thought the world of him and I have always liked him. I don't know about Guard Swan. He's a Sergeant now and we all know what happened with him and Dixie. Let's give him a day to remember though. He deserves it."

Uncle John got up and said,

"Mary's right. Miley is his friend so he can take him down the village and dress him to the best. It's all on me. Will you do that for me and Mary, Miley?"

"It would give me great pleasure, Sir. Dixie has brightened up all our lives and Michael loved him too. It's probably the least I can do after all the pranks we pulled on him."

"Right," says Mary. "Let's keep it a secret until that day."

Everyone agreed. Uncle John called Miley to one side and gave him a hundred pounds. "While you're there, I want you to dress yourself as well."

"That's very kind of you, Sir. Thank you very much."

"Your Dad saved my Brother's life and I will never forget that. Your family is going to have the biggest house in the village. I'm going to build it myself in the New Year."

Miley couldn't believe such kindness; life was looking up for everyone involved.

Mary was getting very anxious now. Michael was due home on Monday. Everyone went to Mass that Sunday and the church was packed. Father Pat helped Father Tony say Mass. Father Tony got up on the pulpit and gave a beautiful sermon.

"Brothers and Sisters, today is the most joyful day in our village. Our brother, Michael Flynn, is alive and well and will be returning home to us tomorrow sometime. After all of the tragedies we have experienced together, something good has come out of it.

It reminds me of a poor Shepherd boy who only had a dozen sheep. One of the sheep went astray so he went and told his Father. His Father said, 'Come with me, Son and together we will find our lost sheep and bring him home to his family'. They searched high and low and were overjoyed when they eventually found him. They brought him home and put him among his flock. He never strayed again. Michael was a lost sheep. He was frightened and had to leave our lives years ago. We gave up on him and when they found a body, his memory was buried with the body. Our good Shepherd, Father Pat has found him and he will be among his own flock tomorrow, never to stray again."

Mary and most of the congregation cried. It was an emotional time for everyone. Some people had their own guilt about Michael other's just a deep sadness. After the ceremony, Mary laid flowers on the graves of James's and David's and the body of the other unknown child.

Father Pat went into Carpenters to ring Michael about the plans for his homecoming. He got through. He would be on the night sailing ship and would be due at the village by ten o'clock tomorrow morning.

It was Monday; the long awaited reunion was about to take place. Mary was so nervous that she couldn't even sit and was still running round doing the last minute preparations. Seamus had a few brandies as the stress was getting to him too. It was only half past eight but every minute felt like an hour to the both of them. Dan and his family arrived at the cottage at about nine o'clock and Dixie wasn't too far behind them. He was like a new man. He looked very smart in his swanky suit. Joe, Sally and Emma were next to come. The cottage was by now full of people.

"God, Pat," said Seamus. "The whole village is done up. Everybody is waiting. It's great to share this kind of happiness with so many people."

There were flags and banners everywhere. Everyone had done their bit.

At about ten o'clock Dixie said he was going off for a while and little Michael wanted to go with him so he brought him. They walked outside the village. He told Michael that he had to gather some wood for his Ma.

"You're not going to collect wood in your best suit, are you?"

"Ah, I have to. Ma will be needing the fire stocked up."

Dixie climbed into the ditch and began pulling at a loose branch. It broke and he threw it out on the road. A car then pulled up, it was Michael.

"Is that our Michael?" asked Helen.

Little Michael ran to the car.

"Hi ye, Mam. Hi ye, Dad."

"Who is that with you, Son?" asked Michael.

"It's Dixie, Dad. Do you not remember him?"

Michael got out of the car and Helen and the children followed.

Dixie was now pulling out another branch.

"Can I give you a hand with that?"

Dixie looked shocked and then it registered. They both threw their arms around one another and then Dixie started to cry.

"Michael, me auld friend. I missed ye."

Michael started to cry as well.

"I missed you a hell of a lot too."

"I never got back me tax rebate after. Remember you told me I would?"

"Well, don't worry," said Michael. "I'm here to look after you. This is my Wife, Helen."

Dixie hugged her.

"God, it must have winked at you too, Michael, the same as Miley."

"What do you mean, Dixie?"

"The eyebrow, remember, in Murphy's field?"

Michael burst out laughing.

"What's he talking about?" asked Helen.

"Oh, I'll tell you later, love. Hop in here, Dixie my friend. We're going home."

When they got close to the village, there was a squad car parked across the road. Michael wondered to himself if something was wrong. He pulled up and the Sergeant went over to him.

"Welcome home, Michael. I'm Sergeant Swan. I've come to escort you and your family home."

Dixie asked if he could go in the squad car with him and Sergeant Swan agreed. He even told him that he would let him turn on the siren. They entered the village and a huge crowd had gathered for Michael's arrival. They were all shouting 'Welcome home' and waving to Michael.

"Can I turn on the siren now, Sergeant?" asked Dixie.

"Of course, Dixie. Hit that button there."

The siren went off and he was delighted with himself.

"Isn't that great, Sergeant? Why are there crowds of people here waving and shouting?" "They're all waiting for you. Do you see them waving?"

"Now, aren't they an awful band of gobshites? Sure, I only went out the road to get wood for me Ma."

Sergeant Swan started laughing. Dixie never failed to make them laugh.

Father Pat heard the siren and ran to his Mother.

"Here he is, Ma. He's coming."

Everyone ran outside the door. The siren stopped and Michael's car pulled up behind the squad car. Mary was trembling and was holding onto the wall for a bit of support. Michael stepped out of the car with Helen and the children and ran towards his Mother. He threw his arms around her and they both started to cry.

"I'm sorry, Ma, for all that I've put you through. I love you so much."

"It's alright, Son. You were just a frightened little

boy. I understand that now. Welcome home, my little wild boy."

She squeezed him one last time and then approached Helen and the kids. It was Seamus's turn to greet his son and there were more tears.

"I'm sorry, Son, for not believing you. I hope you can find it in your heart to forgive me?"

"There's nothing to forgive, Da. Don't be upsetting yourself."

Mary thanked Helen for taking care of her little wild boy and for her beautiful Grandchildren and she then picked the youngest girl up into her arms. She looked just like she did when she was a little girl.

Michael and his Dad were still hugging so Joe and his Uncle John came over to share in the hugs. There were plenty of pats on the backs and smiles. Michael then broke free and went over to Dan and Miley.

"Welcome home, Son," said Dan as they both hugged.

Maggie started to cry her eyes out.

"Miley, in all of these years I've never forgotten you. You'll always be my best pal."

"Me neither," said Miley.

They too had a good hug. Sally and Emma was the last to get their hugs and kisses and when they had finished, everyone gathered in the sitting room. It was very emotional and everyone was in tears. After a few minutes Mary called Helen into the kitchen. She wanted her to carry in Michael's birthday cake. Helen carried it in and everyone sang happy birthday to him. Michael blew out the candles and everyone hugged and kissed him again. They took out the drinks to celebrate.

Dixie was stood only peeping into the sitting room. Mary brought in an extra chair and asked him to sit down. Father Pat carried in another birthday cake with candles on it. This one was for Dixie. Everyone clapped and sang him a happy birthday too. He was elated as he blew out the candles. Then Dixie put the candles into his pocket. Michael asked Dixie if he had made a wish.

"Yes, I did, Michael. I wished for a talking budgie but it is only a wish because I'll never have one of my own."

Everyone felt sad for him. Mary gave Dixie a birthday card with ten pounds inside that everyone had put together for him. Michael called Miley and Dan and asked them to open the boot of his car. They brought the cage into the sitting room and Michael asked Dixie to take off the cover. He did and it was the most beautiful bird he had ever seen.

"It's a parrot, Dixie, for you."

"Does he talk, Michael?"

"Of course, I fucking talk, Dixie."

"Who said that?" asked Dixie looking confused.

"I said it. Down here."

"How does he know my name, Michael?"

"I told him."

"And he's really mine, all mine?"

"He is Dixie. Happy Birthday."

The parrot then began to sing happy birthday to him. Poor Dixie was in another world watching the parrot.

That evening there was a lot of catching up to do and everyone was recalling the old days. They sat and laughed about the adventures they got up to and even Mary saw the funny side when she heard some of the naughty things that her little wild boy had done.

Michael took some photos out of his wallet and began showing them to his Parents. He was pointing out some of his friends in London.

"And that's Jamaican John. He was my Foreman and a very good pal. I'm hoping to bring him over here in the summer to help me build a few houses."

Dixie asked to have a look at the pictures. He looked twice at Jamaican John and then asked Michael if he was really black?

"Yeah, Dixie, he is. He was one of my pals."

"So there really is black babies," he said looking astonished as usual.

Dixie then went over to Father Pat and gave him five pound from his birthday money.

"Father Pat, I want you to give this to the black babies when you go home."

"I will indeed, Dixie. That's very kind of you."

"And will you tell them that I'm sorry for not believing in them?"

"I will, Dixie." Father Pat laughed to himself.

That evening all the men went down to Carpenter's to have a few drinks together. At closing time, they were all drunk. They all left the pub together and Dan, Miley and Joe went off home together in one direction and Father Pat, Seamus and Michael went the other way. Seamus had both of his Sons at each shoulder, each man holding up the other.

"Da, you know it's not good for me as a Parish Priest to be seen drunk by the neighbours."

"Son, tonight we can do what we like so we'll worry about it tomorrow."

They left Michael at his cottage and then proceeded down to their own house. They reached the cottage and Father Pat gave his Dad a hug. "Happy Christmas, Da. You got the best present of all."

"I sure did, Son, and it's thanks to you. You know, Son, I'm glad you didn't take that job in the mill after all. If you didn't become a Priest, you would have never found Michael."

"You're right, Da. The Lord works in mysterious ways."

"He sure does, Son. He brought my family home for Christmas."

HOME FOR CHRISTMAS

ISBN 1-41204847-8